The House That Jill Built

The House That Jill Built

Ethel Carnie Holdsworth

with an Introduction by
Jenny Harper, Fiona Kay Hornby,
Tess McMahon, Barbara Sanders,
and Janet Swan

Kennedy & Boyd
an imprint of
Zeticula Ltd
Unit 13,
196 Rose Street,
Edinburgh,
EH2 4AT.

http://www.kennedyandboyd.co.uk
admin@kennedyandboyd.co.uk

First published by Herbert Jenkins in 1920

Ethel Carnie Holdsworth published under her maiden
name (Ethel Carnie) and with various versions of her
married name.

Front cover image: Ethel Carnie Holdsworth.
Reproduced with kind permission from Helen Brown.

ISBN 978-1-84921-218-2

To the tired mothers of all nations

I affectionately dedicate this book, in the hope that they will open a door for themselves.

Ethel Holdsworth
Long Tail,
Colden,
Autumn, 1920

A story of change – then and now

By Jenny Harper, Fiona Kay Hornby, Tess McMahon, Barbara Sanders, and Janet Swan

Former "mill girl", Ethel Carnie Holdsworth, wrote this book with a clear mission: believing that in reading stories about working people doing what they could to change things, hearts and minds could be turned towards a better society.

In 1910 Ethel Carnie (as she was then) said that the most difficult task "is to teach people to want something better, to sting them into rebellion against poverty, to fire their hearts with a cause". As a passionate reader and regular library user, she knew of the demand for, and influence of, popular fiction and saw this as the way to achieve her dream of a fairer and more equitable world.

The House that Jill Built was her fifth novel, following three books of poetry and numerous stories and articles. And she was well-qualified to address hearts and minds – drawing on her years working in the mill from the age of eleven and her experiences of extreme hardship during World War I, particularly with the working women and war widows of Nelson, Lancashire. Her time spent working in London writing for *The Woman Worker* (an allied publication to *The Clarion* newspaper, both edited by Robert Blatchford) reinforced her qualifications. Blatchford's gift was to be able to write movingly about injustice and inequality and to present a socialist argument clearly. Ethel Carnie may have subsequently fallen out with Blatchford, but during her months in London she had an excellent role model to help her with her craft.

This introduction examines Carnie Holdsworth's aims in more detail, focussing on the portrayal of a greater role for women in society; the representation of her people, demonstrating to readers of all backgrounds, *why* it was that working people (especially women) wanted change; and the dreams that Carnie Holdsworth had for an altogether *new* society.

As a group, we have used these aims as our starting point and from there have drawn out a number of threads we hope will lead the reader into the novel: threads including our own powerful reactions to reading the novel now; whether women still have this need to find time and space to think and so liberate themselves; the setting up of an actual holiday centre for women and how this links to the way "Jill" did it in the novel; and broader visions for social change. It was always likely that we would have this approach: we are writing this introduction as a collective, but with five different voices – as you will hear. We are a group of women who came to the work of this radical woman largely because Carnie Holdsworth lived in a part of the UK where we live or have roots – East Lancashire. The project "Pendle Radicals" led by Mid Pennine Arts, has been the catalyst that helped build our original interest, and we have then added our own particular interests in women's roles, feminism, working-class representation, social change, and the power of reading. We hope one of our threads will draw you to this novel and the inspirational woman who wrote it. A touchstone that we found ourselves asking throughout the project has been "What would Ethel think?" You may conclude as many of us do that for change to occur there needs to be a process along with time and space for re-evaluation.

Ethel Carnie Holdsworth – an inspiration

Ethel's astute political views had such a clarity and resoluteness. I find them so inspiring.

While reading *The House That Jill Built* two questions kept intriguing me.

"What would Ethel think of women's lives today?" And "Are we still 'tired mothers'?"

Although many things have changed for women since Ethel's time and we have seen huge struggles and gains, I wonder when we look closely at the expectations placed on women and the assumptions placed on female gender roles, perhaps not so much has changed – in terms of our overwhelming work load?

As I sit and write this, I imagine Ethel would be quite scathing of the idea of us women being able to have it all, juggling a career and all the responsibilities that come with being the perfect mother and still be expected to be an interesting lover! Perhaps she might rightly ask us, what sacrifices have men made and what new burdens do they bear, that have created so much space, time and energy for women to be able to fit in all these extra modern responsibilities? Is it not still the case that the bulk of the emotional workload of family life rests resolutely on the shoulders of women?

"Women have been taught from childhood upwards, that their part is to suffer and forgive" [ ] that the end and aim of her existence is to meditate on the glories of cooking, sewing and sweeping..." So wrote Ethel in 1913 in a blistering article in *The Suffragette*. Is it any wonder that we still feel exhausted when we are brought up to be the 'givers' in society, without the equal right to take?

It remains the assumption that women have been liberated and therefore shouldn't complain. In the same article Ethel wrote: "virtues, like societies and worlds evolve, change, decay, and give birth to new virtues. The new virtues of women are going to be - truth, however bitter; action instead of passivity; thought on everything under the sun; and above all the right to fight..."

Over a hundred years after this was written, it could be argued that women have only just begun to enter this new era of truth. If we consider the "Me Too" movement, the trials of Epstein and many others like him, there has certainly only very recently been a change to the status quo of 'keep quiet and just put up with it' – a culture women have had to put up with for hundreds of years. And we certainly need continued action and thought, for the battle will not be finished while institutionalised misogyny continues to exist and women still feel unsafe both in public places and in the home.

Are we still tired mothers? Yes! ...and we not only need a break but we also need to demand that men step up and play their part in changing society for the better for women and girls.

Fiona Kay Hornby

Resolutions that follow

In the course of the Pendle Radicals project, I have discovered this amazing woman, Ethel Carnie Holdsworth, and she has inspired me. I found myself identifying with her due to her working-class, socialist background.

This woman was growing up in the late 1800s and was expected to work in the local cotton mills from age 11. And yet she found the time to read widely, go to political meetings at some distance, have the capacity to think and envisage a different social order and write poems and books. I am astounded at her energy and at what must have been going on in her head. I guess she is the product also of the whole working-class movement that created the Mechanics Institutes and educated themselves.

Ethel Carnie Holdsworth wanted us women to get off our backsides and go and do something – be that going out into the beautiful countryside or bring about social change. She saw that need then, and she would still feel it now – causing us to ask ourselves: why aren't we doing something to bring about social change now when we are surrounded by a dysfunctional society (as she was)? A dysfunctional society which has few winners and a multitude of losers.

Our class-based society concentrates power into the hands of those who are born into privilege and brought up to believe they can effect change. Those not born into privilege can feel powerless: and those feelings of powerlessness sap our energy to believe that things can be different.

At the time Ethel Carnie Holdsworth was writing, it is not coincidental that the Holiday Fellowship was founded - in 1913. This organisation aimed to enable working-class people to escape from overwhelming, impoverished life and step back, breathe, and engage in stimulating discussion. In *The House that Jill Built* Ethel Carnie Holdsworth creates a physical space where women can take that crucial step back and look at their lives, to meet others and compare notes. Could this also be a mental space - a chance to breathe - as a first step to empowerment and demanding a life worth living?

Barbara Sanders

Giving the reader space for change

In this story of a young woman attempting to do good, what is it about Carnie Holdsworth's style that creates space for thought, and thus helps the reader move to a point of greater feeling or understanding, so that they might also be spurred into action to make changes or do good?

The action starts in a damp London bedsit with the smell of burning peas drifting up the stairs from the landlady's flat. But this is going to be a story that will move and change quickly (and this too is an important device to keep the reader engaged), for even though the fact is whispered, Jill has come into money and has plans to change her life. Her initial view of this change is linked only to a better marriage. Writing home she says:

"I have come into a fortune! I am going to be married. I am so happy."

Then she stopped.

The reader too is forced to stop. And reflect: surely the linking of these three things is a dream too far, even if only because the reader has read the title of the first chapter - "Jilted". Of course there will be a romantic element to this story – Carnie Holdsworth's novels were promoted in this way: she understood the desire for escapist fiction for women, which continued to grow in popularity during and after the war years as women sought out escapist literature to help them deal with the horrors of war and then life alone in this new world where women outnumbered men. Her mission, as we have seen, was to use such fiction to help women see that there was a different way.

Having given the reader a sense of recognition, interest and pace plus a story that might be relevant to their own concerns, Carnie Holdsworth then has to create a believable central character who might lead them on this journey of potential change. The "Jill" we meet in the first chapter is familiar – a "country girl" living in the city (the reality for millions of women at the time) – but also a figure to aspire to - reflective, sensitive, insightful – while also being portrayed, through her determination to see "the other woman" in this jilted scenario, as a character not to be messed with (a feature common to Carnie Holdsworth's heroines). But before she becomes these things (even within the space of the first chapter) she is portrayed in a very different way that again might give the reader a reason to reflect:

When her fiancé arrives (and before she knows the purpose of his visit) we read:

She swept up towards him like a tiny whirling wind [ ], lifting her face for a kiss, whilst her whole look said "Shall I please thee, Critic."

By the end of the chapter the reader understands that this is a woman of "grit, grace and gumption", with a vision for change and a plan for what she can now do as a single woman, but not before the reader is given pause for thought about something totally familiar: the way women behave (or used to behave) when in the presence of men – the reality of the sexual type-casting above that can ultimately be seen as slavery. This is a shift that the reader too may need to make, but there will be a process, and it is this that is at the heart of the novel.

With such shifts and thinking points even in the first chapter, the reader knows that they can enter a journey with this writer. This author is a safe pair of hands who has experienced, who understands, and who will create space for the reader to move towards a new way and a new vision.

Janet Swan

A Shining House on a Hill

In *The House That Jill Built*, the eponymous Jill envisages a socialist utopia for tired mothers, a "house on a hill", populated by pioneering "Firstlings". Carnie Holdsworth's notion of a prototypal ideal society bears close and intriguing comparison to another community of "Firstlings". Puritan John Winthrop delivered a now famous speech in 1630 as his fleet prepared to sail across the Atlantic on their way to establishing a New England and a new nation. His important treatise foresaw this new community as a New Jerusalem. "For wee must consider," he sermonised, "that we shall be as *a city upon a hill*". The Puritans' conception was of a new Zion, a new chosen land, a new revolutionary society built upon a hill, much as the one that Jill foresaw. Indeed, these notions are buried deep within the socialist movement, as Barbara Taylor noted in *Eve and the New Jerusalem*: "Owenite lecturers", inspired by the famed social reformer Robert Owen, "frequently referred to Socialism as the New Jerusalem or the Promised Land". These seemingly disparate threads can be tied even closer together, since instructively, socialist and Labour leader Clement Atlee's winning campaign slogan during the 1945 election spoke of "Building a new Jerusalem". His stirring rhetoric and aspiration secured him a landslide victory.

Within US politics, the image of a "city upon a hill" has become a repeated parable, conveying for a series of US presidents the ideology of America as a shining light for the world. The words in Carnie Holdsworth's novel find an intriguing echo. In the book's dedication she talks of the tired mothers she seeks to bring to a kind of Promised Land. She hopes that they will "open a door for themselves", and within the main text, her character Jill presciently speaks of how her house will allow her, "to open a door leading out of all the grey misery into where it is green and happy". President Reagan in his 1989 farewell speech to the nation revisited Winthrop's "city on a hill" ideology, recounting how he'd, "spoken of the shining city all my political life", and expounding on its inclusivity, of how, "if there had to be city walls, the walls had doors and the doors were open to anyone with the will and the heart to get here". The liberating imagery of open doors, of a welcome to all, emerges compellingly as a powerful and recurring trope.

In a final gleam of this continuing thread, Carnie Holdsworth dedicates her book "affectionately" to "the tired mothers of all nations", calling to mind a famous speech by US president Barack Obama. In 2006, Obama employed the familiar "hill" motif in his commencement speech at Boston's University of Massachusetts: "In the most diverse university in all of New England, I look at a sea of faces that are African-American and Hispanic-American and Asian-American and Arab-American", he observed, "I see students that have come here from over 100 different countries, believing like those first settlers that they too could find a home in this City on a Hill". A community of nations indeed just as the one Carnie Holdsworth foresaw.

Carnie Holdsworth was of an age familiar with scripture, and is likely to have had an awareness of the socialist philosophies around the idea of a New Jerusalem, of a new moral world. After all, only two years before *The House That Jill Built* was published, *Jerusalem* had become the official Women Voters' hymn. As both a political radical and a strong advocate for social reform, she would have been aware of both

William Blake's poem and the contemporaneous hymn, and perhaps felt its influence and responded to its implicit imagery in her writing.

The resonance of her ideology within American politics may appear coincidental, however her writing can be seen as gesturing towards a utopian vision. Her model of a democratic and comradely ideal society, with doors open to all, and inclusive of all nations, still exists as an aspirational goal. The ideal remains the same, whether for a fledgling socialist community or for a burgeoning nation. Certainly, they both seek to provide a pioneering beacon of *hope on a hill.*

Jenny Harper

A real-life "house on a hill" (The Women's Holiday Centre) and a way forward

As we have seen, 1920s Jill is passionate about her project: "to build a house on a hill...for tired mothers." She had been left £10,000 with conditions, not all initially disclosed to her.

In real life in 1979 a group of women in the north of England were similarly passionate about a proposed project: "We want to set up a holiday centre for women to have affordable safe holidays...." said a group of women in 1979, one of whom was able to make a donation of £30,000 from a house she had been bequeathed. She didn't want to take individual control, so from the start the search for a suitable house was carried out by a group of women working together. Women and children have visited the Women's Holiday Centre, in the Yorkshire Dales, ever since, all year round (with a pause because of Covid).

While both projects came to fruition, there are striking differences in the context, reflecting the times of each. For the fictional Jill, it was very much an individual project that she carried through by individual drive and determination. Individual men whose input she needed were persuaded to support the project, and women who visited joined in. However there was little sense of a movement of which she was a part, in relation to this project for which Jill had very practical aims to give a break to mothers experiencing poverty, overwork, exhaustion and violence.

Ethel Carnie Holdsworth herself had ample lived experience of family life and working conditions for women in factories, where unionisation, mutual aid and socialism provided a means of working with others to improve conditions. However they reflected a male perspective, whether benign or otherwise. When it came to actual male violence in the domestic sphere, socialism didn't have all the answers. On the contrary male socialists were perfectly likely to be perpetrators of control and violence within the home, backed up by societal norms. Ethel Carnie was well aware of suffragette and suffragist aims and campaigns, and a good number of women active in these movements who came to prominence, such as Selina Cooper and Ada Nield Chew, also lived in Lancashire.

In the 1980s, when the Women's Holiday Centre was being established, there was a supportive, if mixed, context of the Women's Liberation Movement, feminism, gay, lesbian and bi-sexual rights, women's refuges, collective and co-operative ventures, anti-hierarchical organising, green and left political organising, and much more; the lived experience of many of us who were involved. This gave a bedrock of establishing a more collaborative project, with clear ideology, principles and procedures. That is another narrative to tell elsewhere.

Women's spaces, including holiday centres, are still needed and valued in the 21st century, as places of safety, positive shared experiences and campaigning. Male violence against women is still a huge issue. The political, cultural and ideological environment continues to develop, and the points of growth and friction may have changed, but women still need "The House that Jill Built."

Tess McMahon

CONTENTS

CHAPTER I

JILTED

"I THINK," said Jill's landlady, arms akimbo, regarding the only lodger she dared to borrow from with maternal pride, "if he isn't pleased with *that,* he's a hard-to-please young man."

Jill smiled.

She knew that she looked well. But she could not throw off the atmosphere of funeral versus gipsy-carnival, derived from her inner knowledge that this muslin had hung round her grandmother's last bed, after having been before that a bazaar frock. It made her want to laugh and cry. But, then, Jill had a drop of Irish blood in her.

"A bit of good matteral," said Jill's landlady, feeling at the sleeve of the dress.

Jill grew nervous lest the grubby thumb should leave a mark.

"Oh lor, *my peas*!" gasped Mrs. Greenwall, and fled. A smell of burning came up the stairs with their fraying oilcloth.

Jill was too "fey" this night to be sympathetic about the peas. As a rule, she was very sympathetic, the kind of girl who got all sorts of queer confidences from the oddest people. Her father, now dead, had said the child would grow up with a "dilated heart."

Now that Mrs. Greenwall was gone Jill sat on the bed. There were one or two stars to be seen from the window that looked on London from the musty, fusty bedroom of the little typist. Jill looked from the stars to the one beautiful picture in the room, one she had purchased—a mother worshipping a dimpling, gurgling baby.

She took the candle, lit it and walked impulsively to that picture.

It was a silly thing to do, to talk to a picture.

But Jill was only eighteen, and something had withheld her from reposing too much confidence in Mrs. Greenwall.

"I have ten thousand pounds," she said tiptoeing up to the picture. "I am rich; and I am going to be married. I am rich—and happy—and—beautiful!"

She drew herself up, and pursed her mouth at the mother and baby. Then, with a little laugh that she should have told it to them, she walked over to the mirror, holding up the candle. Jill's assertion that she was beautiful was justified to-night. Joy of life made her features radiant. She had done with the old office with the blue gauze blind. She had come into a fortune only that morning. Which only meant—that Harry would have a way cleared to his ambition.

Restless, she waited for him. They were going to a dance. He did not know that she was an—heiress!

Jill sat down in an attempt to write to Mandy. Whilst she wrote she thought of Mandy and Giles, in their quaint farmhouse in Breezeton; Mandy knitting, Giles making pipe-lights, and the silence around it from the hills.

Quite suddenly Jill realized that at the bottom of her heart she was a country girl, though she had worked in London two years.

She drew quite near to Mandy—her face softening, as she wrote:—

"Dear Aunt Miranda,—I have come into a fortune! I am going to be married. I am so happy—"

Then she stopped.

It sounded a selfish letter. Chin on hand; she pondered. Had she got selfish lately?

It was rather a long time since she had written to her people. She thought of Mandy looking over the white gate for the hobbling postman and her eyes filled with tears.

Somehow—Harry had filled her whole world even to the exclusion of her own people. For a year—

She brushed the tears away, tore up the letter and started again:—

"Dear Aunt Mandy,—Forgive me for not writing. I have been a little beast—but indeed, I love you, though the love did not get into my pen-nib. Never mind. Love does not depend on ink. Oh, Aunt Mandy, I saw cherry-blossom to-day. And I was just seven when I looked—and coming to see you, with Dad, on the old spring-cart.

"How is Uncle Giles?

"Tell him I'm coming soon. Is Neddy alive yet? And how are all the people at Breezeton? But—I'm coming soon. Aunt Mandy, I'm going to be married, and I'm coming to spend my honeymoon with you and Giles, and—I want to see Dad's grave. Love and kisses to you both, and—*please* don't think I did forget you, though I didn't write. Though London is a place that makes people forget what they should most remember. It does, Mandy. A good-night kiss, and—God bless, from

Your loving niece, *Jill*."

At the end she realised that she had not told them of the fortune. Writing to these quiet people she had forgotten the money. So she added:—

"P.S.—I have come into ten thousand pounds."

On second thoughts she added:—

"N.B.—Mamma's brother died last week."

She had barely slipped this into an envelope when Mrs. Greenwall's voice floated up the stairs.

"Miss Jill! Your fian-cer!"

Which made Jill want to laugh and shudder. The laugh was for herself, the horror was for Harry's ears.

"Coming, Mrs. Greenwall," called Jill.

The happy, youthful voice penetrated to that room which Jill had dusted only two hours before.

The occupant felt nervous as he heard it, as he stared at the fire newly lit in his honour.

Harry Thorn was a handsome man, of the "boy" type, and he was genuinely, horribly *sorry* for Jill.

She was coming down to go with him to a dance— and he was waiting to tell her, some how, for he *must,* that he wanted his "freedom", that it had all been a sad, impulsive mistake, that life was not romance, but sound business, and he was to marry Sarah Wheeler who had freckles and five hundred pounds.

He heard her on the stairs.

Why, yes—it would not be such a difficult business! Jill was a soft little thing.

He stared wretchedly about the room. It was hideous—save for the touches Jill had imparted to it; her book, her white gloves, the bowl of yellow jonquils. Mrs. Greenwall had not made the supper! Jill had made it. Her dainty mark was on it. Poor Jill. How she loved him!

He screwed up his courage. In a moment she would be in the room. This time he must tell her.

Twice he had come to tell her, and gone away—a coward.

The door creaked. "Oh—Harry!" said Jill.

She swept up towards him like a tiny whirlwind in spotted muslin and a red rose, lifting her face for a kiss, whilst her whole look said "Shall I please thee, Critic?"

"It's all right, Jill," he said, and somehow dodged the caress.

If only the bad business was over!

"I've been dying for evening," said Jill, rapturously. "The typewriter *would* dance! Isn't trifle made of apple—banana—sponge-in-milk, moulded into the shape of a hedgehog, just lovely?"

She took the bowl from the table and held it for his inspection, then smiled up into his face. He experienced the anguish of a young butcher about to kill his first lamb.

"The almonds represent the spikes!" she explained.

Then she set the bowl on the table, and perched herself on the edge beside it. She had always reminded him of a kitten who could not possibly grow into a cat.

"I've—great news, Harry!" she said.

He looked at her.

That sitting on the table habit was her most Jillish attitude.

Fear seized him. He must tell her this time. For, as a matter of fact, he had taken his freedom. Sarah Wheeler had accepted him. His position was untenable, even— to himself.

"Jill," he began.

"Harry," she mimicked.

"I've some bad news," he began, whilst his start sounded absurd.

"O-o-o!" said Jill, jumping from her position on the table. "Not—your mother isn't worse, Harry?"

She was more bewitching than ever with that anxious look deepening her beauty—suddenly solemnized into a brown-eyed owl.

He shook his head.

"How you frightened me!" she said.

He grew afraid of her—her spell upon him. He had sold her and himself for five hundred pounds, and a deal was a deal. His fear of her made him rash, and unnecessarily harsh.

"Jill," he said, "I—I came here to-night to ask you to set me free."

Jill's face was a study. She stared at him as though he had gone mad, or as though she must be.

"Free!"

She repeated his word in a way that made him want to shake her in his misery.

He nodded. Pale-faced, he averted his eyes from hers.

"Free!" gasped Jill. "You mean—to—break off the—"

She stopped. Her bewildered gaze met his.

She was alabaster-white. One little hand plucked at her gown.

"You mean—*that*!" she queried, suddenly, sharply.

He nodded.

"Why?"

She was trembling from head to foot. But her eyes met his with something besides pained interrogation in them. A new Jill, Jill he had not suspected abode in that slight body, flashed forth.

He did not answer.

She sat down.

"You have tired of me?" she queried.

He burst into protestations.

"Please, Harry," she said, simply, "tell me."

The Jillish simplicity became an awful thing to the young man in this moment.

So he started to tell the story—of his father's difficulties and Sarah Wheeler, Jill occasionally bringing him back from meanderings whereby he sought to make it picturesque. He had the old fancy that she was stripping all his draperies from the story, seeing it bare, as it was, and shivered once.

Jill's face went whiter and whiter.

"You—you are faint, Jill!" he said.

"We don't faint," said Jill wearily.

He looked at the drooping figure, and struggled with the temptation to take her in his arms.

"I—she can never be what you are to me, Jill," he said, striving to give comfort.

Then and there Jill rose up.

The astonished young man beheld indeed a "Daniel come to judgement"—a five-foot Daniel in a dancing-dress, with a white face and a cloud of dusky hair and a red rose. Jill's voice was very low, but she did not spare. She summed up the evidence—was judge and jury, and accusing counsel—giving out basic facts in a way her dead father would have relished.

"To think," she wound up, with a burl of Celtic fire that made her like a young priestess "that I have wasted six months of my life nursing such a viper in my bosom!"

"Jill!" he pleaded. Jill smiled.

"If it had been a million," she said, calmly "there'd have been dignity in it! But a few hundreds! To have loved a man *first,* given him *first* place, and then not to weigh against a few hundreds. Why—you win five hundred pounds—with a Limerick!"

Her shaky little laugh told that her limit of endurance was almost reached.

"I tell you—it's not just the money!"

Harry Thorn twisted miserably.

Who would have thought Jill had all that in her? To have seen through it all—all through him.

"You mean—you like her, too?"

"I think," he said, "after what I have seen, that Miss Wheeler will be infinitely more suited to me than——"

Jill laughed again.

"You know, Harry," she said, "you dislike the office work, and this opens the door, and, compared to your ambition, neither Miss Wheeler nor I count. But—such a beggarly sum!"

"The teapot, miss," said Mrs. Greenwall's voice.

She looked inquisitively from one to the other, as she tiptoed to the table. Then——

She could not restrain herself.

"Has she told you the good news, sir?" she asked. "Oh—could she keep it? No, not she. I said, 'You'll out with it as soon as you sees him, an' you'll have to beg on him not to give you up. They always give you up in love-tales when you comes into money!'"

Young Thorn stared at Mrs. Greenwall as she set the teapot down. Had everybody gone mad? What was the woman talking about?

He looked at Jill.

She was trying to smile, trying to sit straight up on her chair.

Mrs. Greenwall smiled herself out of the room.

"Has she been drinking?" asked Harry.

Jill eyed him coldly.

"No," she said. "It's true. My Uncle Birch died suddenly a week ago, and left me ten thousand pounds. I only got to know this morning."

The rest was an increase of the nightmare to Harry Thorn. He went out, like Shylock of old, bewailing equally the loss of Jill—and ten thousand pounds.

As for Jill——

She put on her coat and rushed off to the nearest Tube to see Sarah Wheeler. She eventually found herself in the presence of a plain young woman with a shy manner, who grew more shy as Jill spoke.

"Is it true," asked Jill, "that a Mr. Harry Thorn has proposed to you?"

Her heart was thumping wildly.

"Yes," said Sarah Wheeler.

Jill's suspicion was correct.

She grew sick—sick to think she had been so belittled, that the plain woman had been so belittled, that the generous old earth was trodden by men like these.

"Thank you," said Jill, smiling stiffly.

"And—you will tell Mr. Thorn I called, won't you? He will understand. I'm a—kind of relative! I wish you much happiness, you poor thing!"

She was going down in the lift when Sarah Wheeler recovered from her astonishment at the apparition and its disappearance.

Jill crept along the Tubes. The white shining tiles of the rounded walls dazzled her eyes. She had a feeling that burning sand was behind them. Once or twice she paused, a strange heaviness about her feet, wondering if she might faint, then rallying to the tradition that no Bennett had ever fainted.

People looked at her strangely. It was all a world of dream, this London—a bad, bad dream, where life was sordid, where men set a few hundred pounds against a girl's heart—where deluded women, like poor Sarah Wheeler, accepted men who had already sweethearts.

"I just hate men! sobbed Jill, when she flung herself on her bed and the rain of tears came down, leaving her a tossed wreck, shaken from time to time by a great sob.

Being a little Irish, Jill could hate very well, for a girl of eighteen. But the awful blow was to have loved a man—so *mean!*

Her next week was one of utter demoralisation. There was no work to go to. She had given it up. Uncle Birch's lawyer had sent a hundred pounds to go on with.

She went as far as Kensington Gardens once. The trees were leafing nicely. The sun and shadows played under the great trees. She sat and watched the children, and walked round to see Peter Pan and his admiring group of children. Mothers and children. Everywhere she saw them. And now—she should never have any children, she who had possessed a dream-house of her own at forty years of age, and quite a little family!

One day she took a wild whim to go down into the East End. Jill's shock had given her a critical turn of mind. She suspected that half the things she had believed in, as well as Harry, were illusions. She had heard the poor spoken of almost as if they were a different race from those "genteel" workers in offices, and from those Kensington Gardens middle-class mothers, who took the children to see dear little bronze Peter, play his bronze pipe, until the rabbits came out of their holes to listen to him, whilst the daffies danced on his little green hill.

Jill sampled Bethnal Green, Bow, and Poplar. She trudged their by-streets, their open-air-markets, breathed their greyness, realized the unutterable miles of it all, soaked its ugliness in at her pores. Then she went to see her Uncle Birch's lawyer.

"Well?" he queried, benignly.

"Can I have all that money when I like?" asked Jill.

"There are no conditions about the ten thousand pounds," began the solicitor, then pulled himself up in time.

Jill was such a child in appearance, people often said things they didn't mean to in her presence.

He had almost told her of that other clause of which she was not to know for three years, unless—

"I want to build a house," said Jill.

"Very nice," he smiled.

Jill had not got over the fancy that she had to explain why she wanted the money in order to get it, as though it came out of her solicitor's pocket.

"For Tired Mothers," said Jill, dreamily.

"Eh?" said Mr. Wicks, readjusting his spectacles.

She was the maddest client he had ever had.

"I am going," affirmed Jill, "to build a house—on a hill—for Tired Mothers. I am going to open a door leading out of all that grey misery into where it is green and happy. Do you know of an architect, Mr. Wicks, sufficiently on the ideal side to be worthy to build such a place?"

She was drawing the plan of it on Mr. Wicks' table with a ruler whilst he stared at her.

"Do you mind telling me what you mean by 'out of all that grey misery'?" he asked, mildly. He was wanting to decide whether it was wise to bring Will Mason and Jill together like this—whether it kept to the letter of the will.

So Jill told him of her trudges in the East End.

"You shouldn't go there," he told her, shaking his head.

Jill's eyes met his.

"They—live there!" she said.

Her simplicity became again that awful weapon Harry Thorn had felt.

"Er—yes—my dear; but—" began Mr. Wicks.

"I am going to give those mothers a holiday," said Jill.

"*All* the mothers?" smiled Mr. Wicks.

Jill winced this time.

"I wish I could," she murmured, and tears came into her eyes.

"Your heart does you credit," said paternal Mr. Wicks, "but I am afraid your head—"

Then Jill laughed, in her way that told of the little drop of Irish blood that goes such a long way.

The sepulchral-voiced clerk opened the door.

"Mr. Mason!" he announced.

Jill rose to go.

"Wait a moment," said Mr. Wicks, making his decision. "I believe, Miss Bennett, here is your architect."

CHAPTER II

JILL REVIVES

THE door of Mr. Wicks's office was opened so impetuously that Jill felt sure that the plain young man who entered must have heard the old man's remarks.

"William, this is the niece of your friend Birch," said Mr. Wicks, adjusting his spectacles and beaming at the plain young man in an unlegal way.

Jill was conscious that the plain young man stared at her in a surprised manner—stared so long that she felt he was rude, when Mr. Wicks observed, "Miss Bennett, Mr William Mason—your uncle's one great friend."

Jill found her hand seized in a large one that almost swallowed hers. The grip hurt. They discussed the weather.

Then Mr. Wicks said: "William, sit down. This young lady thinks of building a house. She asked me if I knew of an architect, and I had just recommended you."

It was at this moment that a knock fell on Mr. Wicks's office door, which slowly opened, to reveal the face of the white-haired clerk.

"Mr. Wicks, Mrs. Wicks is mounting the steps," he said, gravely.

Mr. Wicks was suddenly transformed into a worried, nervous old man.

"I'm coming, James," he said.

At the door he half-turned and looked at the couple whom his strange client had set down in the codicil as to inherit his vast fortune if—they would marry each other.

Jill was enthusiastically describing her Dream House to young Mason. That plain young man was listening. His plain eyes expressed quite keenly to Mr. Wicks that he scarcely thought Jill a suitable person to be out mothering the mothers.

But he was very respectful, as before a person who would give him a "job."

Mr. Wicks closed the door gently behind him.

"Poor Wicks!" said young Mason, half-smiling, half-tender. "He has married a second time." Then, as Jill stared, he added: "She's jealous."

They could hear poor Mr. Wicks talking to his "better half."

"Have you seen Halgrove Chambers?" queried Mason, alluding to the Chambers Uncle Birch had left to Jill.

She shook her head.

She was listening in a pained way to Mr Wicks apologizing to his wife for imaginary grievances.

"Come along and let me show them to you," said young Mason. "I live in the same block. That's how I got to know your uncle. Oh—the key!"

"I have it in my bag," said Jill.

She had carried it about a whole week without the desire to see her possessions.

They passed Mr. and Mrs. Wicks on the stairs.

She gave Jill a fierce scrutiny, but after a glance at the plain young man grew more mild.

"What—how did you subdue her?" sail Jill, when they were out of earshot.

The plain young man smiled. Quite suddenly he ceased to be a plain, young man.

"I've a great will," he said, jestingly "Perhaps she felt it. Wireless, you know. When I was a boy, at home, I once went to a wild-beast show, and was looking at a lion. It suddenly began to roar. I had to go away. The lion was antagonized. That is how I discovered that for one person with a will like mine there are ten thousand who haven't it."

He was still smiling.

"I wish I could lend Mr. Wicks a little of it," he said, boyishly rueful all at once. "I've so little need of it, you see. Life flows on like that for me."

He moved his hand, making a straight line in the air.

"You never know what you'll need," said Jill, seriously.

As she looked up at him he caught a full view of the face, with its impulsive mouth, dreamy eyes, and stubborn chin—a flash of the Jill who was nineteen parts English, one part Irish.

"You never know," he admitted.

They took a taxi.

When it stopped before a pile of grey mansions, with trees growing in the Square, and only echoes from the big London filtering to them like the sounds of drops of water pattering into a deep, deep well, Jill said: "Oh, what a lovely place! I shall leave Mrs. Greenwall's!"

The caretaker opened the hall-door, nodded to Mason, and looked curiously at Jill. He coughed all the way up, talking Devon vernacular to Mason.

Then—

"Here we are," said Mason.

Jill stood before a heavy oak door, curiously carved, and deep-sunken.

This was where her strange uncle had spent twenty years of his life, where he had spent two years since she came to the City after her father's death. He had never seen her since her childhood. He had never invited her to the Chambers. But—he had left her his den, and ten thousand pounds. She had a feeling that she was dreaming.

Then—she fumbled in her bag for the key.

"Let me help you!" said young Mason.

In the helping they got a little mixed, and something fell out on the green mat. Young Mason bent and picked it up, holding it out to Jill. It was a pendant, with a young man's face staring out of it.

"Thank you!" said Jill.

She blushed, without knowing why she did it, and bustled Thorn's picture back in her bag.

Looking at her a moment later Mason saw that she was quite white.

Houses for Tired Mothers—miniature of young man—living for the world—!

He drew his own conclusions.

They were pretty accurate.

And he smiled that robust, inward smile that was without either pity or cynicism, the smile that had sweetened with its human faith even in human folly the last years of that strange old bachelor who had lived so long behind this frowning oaken door.

Jill threw back the door.

Then—

"You first," she said, childishly.

Quite suddenly she felt that she believed in ghosts—not apparitions, but memories of people clinging to places where they have lived.

Mason went first. He did not laugh.

Jill followed him—stepping into a large room whose windows and furniture were shrouded. It was Mason who uncovered them—almost as if uncovering the dead.

Jill stared into a room in which the walls were almost covered with pictures.

"Mr. Birch had a beautiful soul," said Will Mason, gently.

Jill could believe it.

Then—

"And—to think of the awful hand-painted Christmas card and the socks I always sent him!" she said, with sudden vision.

"That," smiled Will Mason, "was why he left you these chambers. He said that ugly little duck, followed by the consumptive bird, and the freak pansies, and the green silk socks with the heels too small, were the only human touches in his life. I honestly believe: those things, and the fact that you never *asked* him to let you see him, did it. Little things—but a lot depends on them—sometimes."

Jill wandered round the chambers.

Everywhere pictures—pictures of sand-dunes, seascapes, exquisite water-colours, flushed the walls into reflections of the beautiful earth.

Jill thought of Bethnal Green—the greyness, the hardness of the streets, the bargaining for meat, fish that made its presence audible, the huddled houses where life came into a world of ugliness, only redeemed by one beauty—Love, human Love. She thought of the mothers, as she looked at these reminders of the beauty of the earth.

Something of this she told to young Mason. He ceased to regard her as quite so much of the irresponsible he had taken her for. And with the thought came the other tantalizing one regarding the picture that had fallen from her bag. Was there, under the irresponsibility of Jill, a deep under-woman, who would remember to her grave, and — live out her virginity, loving only the big human family? Which worried him rather. Because—he was thinking unarchitectural things. Of Jill's eyes.

But when Jill had made the fire, and lunch, Mason showing her where all the things were, he had forgotten it.

He told her a little about himself—his work, and that he was under the guidance of Sir Christopher Jones, the famous architect. In the middle of luncheon Jill described her ideas of the house she wanted building.

"But—where?" asked Mason, smiling.

Jill's eyes were gazing dreamily at a little etching over the fireplace.

"There!" she said, popping a morsel of cake in her mouth.

Mason followed the direction of her finger. He saw a great hill—and a valley, with a river, and shadowy trees, and cows.

"That's home—my home, Breezeton," said Jill. "But it's not grey, like the etching, it's green, and green and gold and white in the summer, and there are old lanes, with dog-roses, and moors near, with sea-winds blowing in on them. That's where I'm taking my mothers. Besides, Aunt Mandy could help me." She told him of Mandy and Giles, not really her aunt and uncle, except by adoption.

As she spoke softly of them she leaned her chin on her hand. Whereupon young Mason began to make up his mind more quickly than ever he had done in his life. But all that he showed outwardly was a cool attention to all Jill said about Firstlings Hill, and he discussed with her the difficulties and advantages of hill-top architecture, folding up Jill's rough drawing of his Dream House, and putting it inside his pocket book in a very businesslike way.

When he had gone—

Jill realized that it was hardly convention to send a young man out for tinned apricots on a first acquaintance.

"Cupid Brand"—with two little Cupids on the outside tin, sitting on plump, yellow apricots!

He had poured tea out for her, too, while she spoke of the Dream House.

Meanwhile—

In that room of his own, where he kept his few treasures, young Mason was depositing Jill's drawing. He placed it in a queer place for a business document— within the glove, tucked cosily inside his mother's bridal wreath of artificial orange-blossom and silver leaves.

He heard Jill leave the place half an hour later, and took a peep from the window.

She had a queer, characteristic walk.

He watched her out of sight.

Then he heard the caretaker coughing his way up the stairs.

"All this lot for you, Mr. Will," said the Devonian. "Love-letters! All love-letters."

He laughed his way downstairs.

Will regarded half-a-dozen envelopes, all in one feminine hand, the gatherings of his ten days' absence from his rooms—all from one Miss Susan James, his cousin, who informed him that she was shortly coming to London. He read them with just a shade less pleasure than usual.

As for Jill—she wanted to kick herself for carrying Harry's photograph about with her still. Mason had made her feel ashamed of it. His robustness had made it seem sickly sentimentality. She wrote to Harry that evening a brief letter, very unlike those she had used to pen—eight sheets long—and the memory of which made her want to die.

> "Dear Mr. Thorn,—Kindly return photograph omitted as yet, also portion of hair belonging to me.
>
> "Yours truly,
> "Jill Bennett."

She dropped Harry's photograph into the fire. She had possessed about ten of him, and did not think he would remember this one.

CHAPTER III

BUYING THE SITE

Jill met William Mason by appointment, a week later, under the clock at Euston Station. They took tickets for Breezeton—third-class tickets.

"You see," said Jill cleverly, "I might meet some tired mothers on the way down, mightn't I, travelling third?"

Eight hours of train travelling did not seem long, for the dream engrossed them both, and at Crewe a fat woman with a baby got into the carriage. She was so "fagged," as she put it, that she did not notice Mason's look to Jill, which plainly said, "Here is a tired mother!"

Jill held the baby whilst she found her ticket. That opened confidences.

She had seven at home. Her mother had had fifteen. Jill was all sympathy.

Which opened the floodgates of mother-trouble, and very soon both Jill and the architect knew the little rough-and-tumble house with the handy husband, and the little lads who *would* fight when they'd gone to bed, and the little girl who went on a crutch, and the great struggle to make ends meet.

Jill told her of the House on the Hill, and she stared as though she heard some fairy-tale.

"Eh, but I couldn't leave 'em," she said, clutching the baby more tightly.

But Jill cajoled her name and address out of her, and promised to write when the House was opened.

"Well, I'm not as bad as one I saw in the paper," said the woman. "*He* read it this morning. She'd nineteen. An' she went to the police-station an' asked 'em to take her in, to give her a rest, for she was afraid she'd commit suicide."

"Which paper?" gasped Jill, excitedly.

"Here it is," said the architect.

As he handed her the paper he had one more unarchitectural appreciation of Jill's beauty.

Jill read the pathetic four-line paragraph. She leaned her chin on her hand.

"It does seem unjust—life—doesn't it?' she asked, pathetically, the weight of a world of tired mothers on her slight shoulders. She took down the address of the unhappy mother of the nineteen.

"Now, it wouldn't take me *that* way," confided the fat woman. "No, not if I'd a hundred. I just picks up one an' knocks the other down w' it, and trusts to the Lord they'll all grow up into folk some day."

She had to get out at the next station. She shook hands with Jill as if she was a deliverer, and Jill said she would not lose the address, and they would be sure to meet again.

After that Jill lay back against the carriage cushions and dreamed.

The human contact with the "tired mother," the thought of that other overburdened one of the nineteen, had fired her with a nobler earnestness. Meanwhile the train was flying through villages and towns, the villages looking like bits of heaven dumped down next to plots of the other kind. They were nearing the North—of moorlands and mills.

A soft, sunshiny glimmer was upon everything as they stepped out on a little platform with spring flowers set on the banks. The brick-workers were coming from Neigham—and stared at Jill in a tired, unenvious way. Jill looked along the platform. She had sent word that she was coming. She was expecting a straight old farmer to meet her.

A bent figure went past her twice, then an old voice said: "Jill? S'cuse me if it isn't, miss. I'm come to meet Jill Bennett."

Farmer Giles and Jill gazed at each other, Jill was the first to recover from her wonder,

"Why, it's really Uncle Giles," she said brightly.

But Mason had seen the gleam of sudden tears.

"Eh—I shouldn't ha' knowed thee out for the eyes," laughed the old man. "The eyes told me. *Them* hasn't changed a bit. Ten years, Jill, sin' thee rolled into th' brook, an my old missus dried on thee!"

"How is Mrs. Giles?" asked Jill.

"Out on her pain, Jill, now," he said, solemnly.

"Oh!" gasped Jill.

She was extremely cautious in asking after anyone else, lest they, too, should be dead. The trio went on down the long lane leading to the village.

"An' this is thy young man, I suppose! Jill?" queried Farmer Giles.

"Oh—dear, no," said Jill, red with confusion. "This is an architect. But I'll explain after tea."

"Nay," blundered the old man, leaning on his stick. "You mun excuse me. Tammie went to London and met a girl worked anest you, an' she said you'd a young man, an' I says, 'Well, if Jill has, she'll bring him—an' he's worth bringin'—an' if he's not she'll noan on him.' I allus said"—turning to the embarrassed architect—"'at Jill wouldn't be caught wi' chaff." Jill was in a fix.

"So you left on him behint, Jill," said Giles, evidently not going to let the question drop.

She could see the subject was going to be an encumbrance, and saw that poor old Giles forgot when he had been answered on a point. She made a bold resolve. For some strange reason she didn't want her travelling companion to know she had possessed a lover who had jilted her. She wanted to satisfy old Giles and stop him from ever alluding to the subject again.

"He—he—died, Giles," said a tremulous little voice in the shadows of the deep lane.

"Died!" said Giles, "died!"

Just at this moment they reached a white gate leading to a trim garden, at the end of which stood a long, low house, whitewashed, holly on each side of its wide door.

The door opened—letting out a flood of fire-glow, and a cheerful voice.

"Has she come, Jim?" called the voice, and a replica of Giles, ten years younger, and feminine, appeared in the doorway. Then the old woman hurried down to the gate. She stared at Jill open-mouthed.

Then lifted up the corner of her apron.

"Eh—but she's grown up bonny!" she said, as if that was something to cry for.

"And this is——"

She looked at Jill's companion.

"No, no," said Giles, hurriedly, "she's buried on him, Mandy."

He had to repeat the statement as his sister was deaf.

They all filed into the red-ochred farm-kitchen, with its Scripture pictures on the walls

"Well, happen it'll be a blessing," said Mandy, suddenly, in the midst of waiting on them at supper. Then as Jill and all looked at her questioningly, she said: "I mean burying on him. An' we'll say no more about it. But it must have been sudden. What was it?"

"Appendicitis," said Jill.

"Like the King," nodded Mandy. "Fancy that, now!"

When Jill looked up and across the table she found Will Mason's gaze fixed on her face. His sympathetic look told that he now quite understood why she wished to build a house for Tired Mothers. And quite suddenly, as she caught that look, she began to cough over a piece of cake. Gracious! The absurd young man thought she was putting it up as a—Memorial! To—Harry—Harry, who was not dead, and who wouldn't have understood her dream in a million years. Jill had regained her sense of humour, and that is always a saving grace, even without courage, of which poor little Jill had her fair share also.

But, for all that, as she lay in the pleasant country room, on the four-poster bed Mandy had made, and the murmur of the wind in the trees came to her, she felt very forlorn—and the idea was so far borne in on her that she was forlorn that she transposed part of the "House that Jack Built."

But when she had got out of bed, and written it down, there were only two lines, and she decided to complete it as the House progressed. Upon the white paper these lines stood forth in Jill's large sprawl:—

"This is the House that Jill Built;
These are the dreams that lay in the House that Jill Built."

When the farm door closed behind the man who was to build her House o' Dreams, as he went to seek accommodation in the Brown Hare, she fell asleep, with less heartache than usual. For Jill had decided that, having told Mandy and Giles that Harry was "buried", she would make it as near true as possible by burying the thoughts of him.

Just after Jill had dropped to sleep Mandy came with her candle. Jill awoke with a start, to see the night-capped sweet old face bending down over her. For a minute it seemed that she was at home again, in the old house her father had practised in, the most beloved doctor in the country. She just felt a very little, little girl—and that she had only dreamed of those difficulties her father got into, not through the wine-cup, as was said, but because he had too much milk of human kindness in him, and cancelled bills, and worked and laboured for a pittance, whilst other doctors claimed big money fees, but never the love that followed that bankrupt doctor's funeral coach.

All that followed was a dream too. Her going to London, to the friend of her father's who had her made into a lady clerk—as a duty perhaps, in payment of a debt.

"Oh, Aunty Mandy !" she exclaimed, "I was thinking—"

Mandy nodded.

"Aye," she said. "The hardest bit for Giles an' me was—we'd to hire ourselves out elsewhere when the tide turned against him. Lean times he'd let noan suffer wi' him. And when little Beatty died!"

They sat and talked, Mandy shading the candle with her wrinkled hand.

Then—out from a drawer came a big, russet apple—just as if Jill was a little girl again, and her twin alive.

Jill stared at it—laughed, the laugh growing shaky. She was surprised to find herself sobbing, dropping great tears on the lavender scented sheets, and the soreness that had clung to her since Harry jilted her faded somewhat and she forgot all the mean young men in the world.

Mandy giving her that apple gave her sacrament without knowing it; Mandy kissing her tears away and dropping some of her own made everything right. Only—Jill felt that she would die before ever confessing to Mandy and Giles that there were mean folk in the world. As the candlelight faded from the rose-sprigged wall that was Jill's last conscious thought.

"Before the break o' day" Jill was up and out, showing young Mason Firstlings' Hill, as the one and only site in the world for her Dream House. In the dewy morning glimmer, with the green of the newly-leafing hawthorns, the bleat of the lambs, the faint gleam from the winding brook at the foot, it made an ideal picture.

The young man went down the hill and looked dreamily up at it.

Jill looked down on him from the top.

"Well?" she called.

He smiled enthusiastically.

Jill found something oddly soothing in the absurd youngness of him. Harry had always made her feel quite small. She had already given Mason motherly advice which he had taken smilelessly.

They set out, after breakfast, to try persuade "old Muggs," as he was known locally, to sell Firstlings' Hill.

As the journey was so long Mandy put their lunch to carry. They ate it outside, hill rising all round them, and young Mason spoke of his little mother in Devon.

As they dropped into Fence a solitary magpie startled Jill.

"One for sorrow," she jested.

"You don't believe—" began her companion.

"I belong to these parts," was Jill's answer. Then she remembered that life had done her worst for her—that she had lost Harry, and they were silent until they came to the farm of the old man who they had been told would not sell Firstlings' Hill for "love or money."

CHAPTER IV

THE ROOF GOES ON

A RED-HAIRED girl of sulky expression led Jill and Will Mason into the kitchen, where her grandfather was eating his dinner.

"I never does business till I've eat," he remarked.

Jill sat down on the old settle under the window, where the blue and white hyacinths were coming up in the brown pots. Mason sat down also.

It was quite twenty minutes before "old Muggs" said, "Now, I'm ready. Come in here."

They followed him into a cheerful parlour.

"What do you want?" he asked, bluntly. Jill's brown eyes met the old farmer's.

"I want Firstlings' Hill, please," she asked as coolly as a child asking for an ice-cream sandwich.

"Eh?" gasped the old man.

"I want Firstlings' Hill," repeated Jill, firmly.

She sat down, propped her chin on her hand, looking at him as though she meant to carry it away there and then.

"I wouldn't sell Firstlings' for a million," said the old man. He appeared stunned, though.

He also sat down, looking at Jill as though he had never in his life met anyone so small with so much assurance.

"I haven't a million," said Jill, "so I couldn't offer it. What I do offer is—five hundred pounds for a hundred years' lease." Which was so sudden and so definite, young Mason gasped.

"No, no," mumbled the old farmer.

"Six hundred"—bid Jill, impetuously. There was silence.

"Six hundred and fifty," said Jill.

"Not—at any price," said the old man. "What have I to sell Firstlings' for?"

He looked at Jill waveringly.

"You pasture six cows there," she told him. "You could pasture them just as well in Long Fields. Six hundred and seventy."

"Old Muggs" rose up.

Jill felt she had lost ground.

It is easier bargaining with a man seated than one who walks about.

"But—I don't want to sell!" he said almost fiercely.

"Seven hundred pounds is a lot of money,' said Jill, "for a bit of a hill that pastures six cows."

The old man sat down.

Then he called, "Nelly, bring the ink."

The red-haired girl brought the ink and a pen that would not write. But Mason had one, and, by bringing in a neighbour the necessary witness was found. Jill was to pay the money down within one calendar month, and left a fifty-pound cheque on account.

When Jill and Mason got back to the Giles' farm Mandy had tea ready and candles lit and a royal fire. After tea Mason played on the yellow-keyed harmonium. They celebrated the capture of Firstlings' Hill for the site of the Dream House by snatches of "Gloria," Jill singing, too, and old Giles nodding his head at Mandy to tell her that Jill was getting over the "burying on him" as well as could be expected!

Jill went back to London next morning leaving Mason behind, to get estimates, builders and work out all details of the house.

It would be six months, at the earliest, before it could be completed. Jill, at her end, was to ferret out people to sit on the management committees—people who could enter into the ideal side of the scheme, and make it the only one of its kind.

She worked strenuously during the next months, and was so particular in her demands that at the end of this time she had only set down the names of six people as "likely." But her list of the mothers who needed to be received in the house o' dreams was so long that she wished she had a dozen houses on hills!

For Jill spent the bulk of her time, when not hunting for a committee woman, down in such places as Bow, Poplar, and Bethnal Green. She took names and addresses in buses, tubes, mean streets, any place, until the heat got on her nerves, It was whilst returning from one of these strange trips, utterly weary, craving for tea, and with a splitting headache, that she met Harry Thorn.

"Jill!"

The sound of her name in the old voice made her heart beat furiously—as it had not done for a long time. She turned, saw him, and paled in excess of emotion. For a moment the old spell was on her, then she nodded a little stiffly, and would have passed on. But this Harry would not allow.

They travelled as far as South Kensington together— and he was asking her innumerable questions about herself, above the rattle of the bus. Whilst she was struck by something superficial and—a little coarse— things she had not noticed in Harry before, and— just for a moment, Will Mason's face, with its almost absurd frankness, came up in comparison.

But it was a shaken Jill who spent the rest of the evening in the old chambers where poor Uncle

Ephraim had pondered on how best to bring happiness into the life of the niece he ever remembered as a mad cap child.

After tea she endeavoured to pull herself together by putting the place into order. It needed it badly. She experienced a dim homely pleasure in sweeping the Morris hearth tiles.

Her head and her heart ached, but Jill made herself complete the task. Then she sank into the depths of the old bachelor chair and fell fast asleep.

She woke in the middle of a confused dream in which she was trying to carry a baby to Firstlings' Hill, only to find that the house was blown away. She was conscious of someone knocking. Then a girlish voice said, "Anyone in?"

"Come in," said Jill, sitting up, and rubbing her eyes and finding the room all dim, and the silver owls on a quaint screen staring at her in the way that sometimes made her want to scream.

Somebody came in.

Jill was conscious of a tall figure in a white coat, and a delicious scent of roses.

"Are you Miss Bennett?" asked the pretty voice.

"H'm, yes——" said Jill.

"I'm Will Mason's cousin Susan," laughed the Presence. "I want to be on your Mothers' Rest Committee. Ooo! Isn't London *hot*?"

Jill got up and lit the two eastern lamps.

"Where's Will?" quoth Susan.

"Oh——Mr. Mason," said Jill, after some thought. "He's busy building the house."

She shook hands with Susan, who said, "I'm a Mason, on mother's side. My name's James. I'm a Kindergarten teacher, on holiday. Now, do you know any nice place where I could go? Don't want an hotel."

For a moment Jill thought of the Greenwalls.

She was sufficiently heartsick not to feel prompted to hospitality—then—"Stay here," she said, a little shyly.

Susan James was rather bewildering.

"Oh—-how splendid!" said the tall girl, "And—I say—couldn't we have the first meeting whilst I'm up? It would be fine! You know, I don't know much about it, except what Will boy has told me. But the idea—and it's ideas that count, isn't it?—it's a glorious idea. And I'm prepared to give every ounce of energy I've got to making it go.'

The superb creature looked it.

"The—the roof isn't on the house, yet, said Jill, haltingly.

"Bother the roof," laughed Susan. "We can form the committee, and make things hum a bit. Newspaper notices and all that sort of thing."

"I can fill it without those," said Jill. She looked at her guest for a few seconds. Then she decided that she liked Susan James. She fetched out all the scores of letters she had received from mothers who had told each other of the scheme—and they read them together.

"Poor, sweet darlings!" quoth Susan. "When they get away from the poverty and struggle, and the children's noise—to say nothing of husbands"—with a ripple of a laugh—"won't it seem heaven!"

"I should like the house to be ready by August," said Jill, "just to give it a trial, this year."

There was much more talk, and dreaming, and youthful scheming to make the house on the hill a success, and Jill began to realize that she had caught a treasure in Susan James, and said so, frankly.

"Well," admitted Susan, who was leaning back in a chair smoking a cigarette, "I don't mind telling you that from being seven years old I can't remember setting my heart on doing anything, or having anything, but I've had it."

For the thirteenth fraction of a second Jill felt that she did not like Susan as she flashed out then. But she told herself firmly that it was prejudice aroused by the cigarette.

It was just before they turned in for the night that Jill was astonished by Susan saying, suddenly, "Oh—Miss Bennett—you don't know that cousin of mine has got mixed up with some woman or other up in your part of the country, do you?"

Jill just stood and stared.

Susan explained.

She was brushing out masses of hair the colour of ripe corn, and her tall figure swayed as she made the onslaught upon it.

"You see," she said, through the hair "Will and I are more or less engaged. Since he's been working on this house he hasn't been quite so affectionate. That's all."

"I don't know anything about his interests", said Jill, flushing. "I'm sure he wouldn't dream of telling me. I just contracted with him to build the house."

Susan tossed herself free of the hair. She answered something that flushed in Jill's eye.

"Oh—don't worry about it," she said casually, "I only thought you might give me the cue. Maybe he's just taken up with the work. It would be the kind of task would lose himself in."

Jill had another of those forlorn feelings that came to her now, whenever she saw a pair of lovers together, however poor they were. This was an unusually keen pang—so much so that Jill wondered as she got in bed if it could be possible that she was cattish enough to envy another woman the admiration of that absurdly young "young man". Another idea flashed on her before she fell asleep. So uncomfortable did it make her in the morning, over breakfast, that she informed Susan that she had been engaged but had "buried" her sweetheart, and would never under any circumstances think of marrying. She perceived that Susan was quite evidently relieved and that she had been right.

Whilst the fact that this was the second lie she had told about Harry being dead made her quite unhappy.

It was so much easier to say he was "buried" than that he had jilted her. In a peculiar, sensitive way she felt she would sooner die than that Will Mason should ever know she had been—*jilted*.

That afternoon the committee was formed. It met in the room where Uncle Ephraim Birch used to smoke his churchwarden.

It was rather young.

That struck Jill at the moment. The eldest member claimed twenty-two summers. All of them were modern. There was a good deal spoken of bringing Art to the mothers. Miss Briggs, who knew a bit about Ibsen, wanted an inscription put up in the "home"— that one where Nora says she is a human being first and a mother after. Jill, who was President, did not approve. Everybody wanted to talk at once. But that was good. So Jill did not call "Order" as firmly as she might have done.

There was quite a lot of sympathy whenever the mothers were mentioned. When Jill told of the woman in the train, Miss Jones, who knew a lot about clinics, grew moist-eyed. When she read out the paragraph of the woman who went to the police-station and asked to be "took" it was a dramatic moment. The committee realized its responsibilities. As for Susan—Will Mason's cousin—Jill admired her more and more.

It was Susan who called the meeting to points of order, and whose clear voice gave the lead on all important questions. It was Susan who took notes— and when they had all gone Jill sat down and looked them over.

Susan's visit lasted a month, well into the middle of July. Before her return to Devon she asked Jill to accompany her to Breezeton to see her cousin. But Jill did not mean to play gooseberry.

Susan came back from Breezeton in good spirits, giving a glowing account of the progress of the house.

Then she hurried away, and Jill, heaving a big sigh, set to work and wrote postcards to each member of the Tired Mothers' Aid Committee, informing them that until the house was finished they might take a holiday. More than that, she kept her eyes open, to find a middle-aged sensible woman who been a mother herself, and therefore knew all about them. At the end of a week she found her—invited her to be on the committee, and made a vow to co-opt her on that committee, or die in the attempt.

She resolutely beat down wild desires to run up to Breezeton and see how the house was looking, though Will Mason wrote letters that made her want to go.

At the end of the third week in August she received word that the house was finished, and could make excuses no longer. She removed, moreover, a misspelt letter from old Giles, in which he said that Mandy would dearly love a funeral card in memoriam of the poor young man who was "buried "!

CHAPTER V

THE MOTHERS ARRIVE

Will Mason was on the platform to meet Jill. She thought his face bore evidence of strain as they shook hands. His manner towards her was just a shade less frank than hitherto, or, Jill told herself, she fancied it.

She asked eagerly about the house, as they went towards Giles's farm.

"Oh—that's all right," the architect told her.

They stole past the farm, round to the hill to see the place before the sun went down.

There were tears in Jill's eyes as she looked up at her dream, proud and beautiful, as it looked down on the valley, with its winding stream, rolling pastures, and the great trees soon to be ablaze with autumn's pomp.

When she entered the wide hall, painted soft blue, blue right from the tiled mosaic to the dizzy topmost height of the last storey, she could not speak.

There, beside a great hall-fire, the mothers who entered, flustered and strange, could rest, until they got their "breath" and were attended to. As they sat their eyes would fall on a huge painting of a Mother and Child—by Rubens. It was all just as Jill had told him she would like it.

Into the great common room, with its easy wicker chairs covered with bright chintz, and the wide Morris grate at which innumerable tired ones could toast their toes—thence into the drawing-room, all silver-grey and white in its decorations, with carpets that seemed more fit to decorate the walls than be walked on.

The kitchen was spacious as an old world one, but modern to a degree, and its several windows looked out on a garden where its vegetables would be amply supplied, by the look of things. Then there was the garden-room, round at the front of the house—where those of the frailer sort could look down on a world of blooming flowers, the windows open to the stairs that would lead down to paths wandering amidst roses, lavender, and thyme.

The bedrooms were almost barrenly plain. But the white of the painted doors and windows, and views from those same window made amends.

But when Jill saw her own room—from which she would ply the reins of gentle government—tears rose to her eyes.

It was very tiny; like a corner to creep in.

The same heavenly blue of the hall-walls was here also—blue that made one think of rare days of June, or the blue of the Gulf Stream.

There was only one picture in it, over the fireplace. It was called "A Rainy Day"—and so beautifully accurate that Jill felt she must get under an umbrella. There was a tiny chair, with fat cushions.

"How could you know I loved a teeny room and blue best of any colour?" she asked.

"I am glad you are pleased," said Mason simply.

Jill trod on air as she went on to the Giles'. Mandy had asked young Mason to come too, and had made a Yorkshire potato pasty in honour of the occasion.

That night, when the first stars shone, Jill and Mason hied forth on a mysterious errand. Jill carried a drinking cup. Mason filled it out of a shining pool in the stream, and they carefully ascended the hill.

They passed in like a couple of ghosts—into the great hall. Therein they lit the first fire. The flames leaped up—and great fantastic shadows danced.

"I am so glad, so glad," Jill kept saying.

Mason did not add anything to this. His task was finished.

By it, though Jill did not know, he had lost five hundred pounds, and—his heart.

When the fire had died down into a dull, red mass of colour Jill took the libation, and standing up, a tiny, fantastic figure in her white dress, said simply, in her girlishly sweet tones, "I dedicate this House to Motherhood—to the Tired and Over-Burdened Souls. May they learn here the joy, the beauty, the meaning of—life."

There was the sound of the water trickling on the hall floor.

"It's over," said Jill, with a laugh in her voice. "I've dedicated—"

Then, how it happened they never could tell, down fell the drinking-cup, and broke into a hundred pieces on the hard tiles of the hearth.

Overstrung as she was by the emotion of the dedicating—Jill screamed.

The girlish scream echoed through the empty rooms.

Mason took her hand in his.

"It was an accident, Jill," he said.

She was shaking like a leaf.

It was only when they stood outside under the stars they both realised that he held her hand still—and that the door was left unlocked. They went back to secure it.

"It—seemed such a bad omen !" said Jill.

She was rubbing the hand Mason had held.

During the rest of her two days' stay Mason was just the same frank boy she had met at first. Only when Mandy was asking about the "burying-card" did Jill feel uncomfortable under his eyes, and wild at herself for blushing. She felt that it was not proper to blush when asked for a "burying-card" of one's dead sweetheart.

She put Mandy off as well as she could.

Jill and Mason travelled homewards together.

It was settled definitely that the Opening of Firstlings should be in a fortnight. During this fortnight Jill saw little of Mason. Once she met him on the stairs, and another time he peeped in at the doorway during the inundation of the committee—and saw Jill, standing on a chair, to be better seen and heard, arguing the point about being able to co-opt a member upon it, if she wished.

Then and there she co-opted Mrs. Briggs, who was large, slow-spoken, and always alluded to herself as "a mother of eight." The airy committee certainly gained ballast from the presence of the common-sense Mrs. Briggs.

All the committee could not go down to Breezeton to be present at the opening, so Peggy Chancer was elected as representative of the moderns, and Mrs. Briggs went as "a mother of eight," and everyone was satisfied.

It was a perfect day in September when Jill, Peggy, the "mother of eight," and the builder of Firstlings met, and travelled north.

The tedium of the journey was beguiled by Jill producing the various letters she had received from various sources—for the venture had been noticed in the Press, and Jill had been interviewed, though she had denied her photograph to the *Daily Sketch*.

The tit-bit of all the correspondence was certainly that from the fogey who asked plaintively why someone did not build a house on a hill for the reception of Tired

Fathers, winding up by denouncing the whole scheme as utter nonsense, and predicting its ignominious failure.

Then there was the letter from the poor woman who said she was not a Tired Mother, but she would be thankful to make pyjamas, if someone would cut them out, and that if she could get this work to do the Lord would bless Firstlings' House!

Mandy and Giles were in possession when the party arrived.

Jill had previously invited all the farmers' wives in the vicinity, and had sent railway fares and full instructions as to route to six mothers, with a copy of the rules drafted out by the modern committee.

The garden party was set for next day, and the six mothers were to arrive in the morning. Contrary to the wishes of all parties, Jill had insisted on Mrs. Briggs opening the House.

The rest of the day, after tea, was spent in showing Peggy and Mrs. Briggs the place—and in getting food supplies in for the occasion.

Jill did not sleep much that night.

She was awakened in the morning by Peggy's gay voice in the garden, followed by the quieter tones of Mason. Peeping from the window, she saw Peggy flirting with Mason, and again was conscious of that "forlorn" feeling. It passed in a moment.

Every moment of Jill's day until noon was filled with work. Cakes, tarts, loaves of bread, jam, arrived in great basketsful—with a quartette of country lasses to wash up the cups, and fetch and carry.

As yet no "tired mother" had arrived.

Mason had been three times to meet trains.

Jill was in a panic.

Fancy opening a house for Tired Mothers, and not one there to show!

In between seeing to the foodstuffs she was instructing Mrs. Briggs on her opening speech.

At one o'clock Mason went again to meet a train. This time two of the Mothers had arrived. Travel-stained, shabby, bewildered, and a little suspicious—Mason ushered them upon Jill in the little blue room.

"Oh!" said Jill, "how tired you must be!"

"It's the first time I've been anywhere," said the eldest, a thin, anaemic woman, "and—we did think we'd never get here."

Her companion, stout, red, and aggressive of look, nodded.

"Mandy!" called Jill. "Tea, please, for these two ladies."

They sat in the little blue room and drank the tea with country cream in it—and Jill smiled—and quite suddenly they became themselves and at home. They went off to wash and "do their hair" in a room they were almost afraid of.

Jill was just finishing writing a letter to Susan James, when there peered in at the door a woman of so nervously abject a look Jill was almost frightened.

"I'm—a—a—mother," said a trailingly tired voice.

"Good gracious!" gasped Jill.

The woman nodded—and looked about as if she did not quite know what she *was* looking for.

Jill set her a chair.

"It was me—I'm the one with the nineteen," said the woman.

She heaved a quiet sigh.

"Mandy," called Jill, excitedly. "Tea," Mandy bobbed in as though she had been waiting round the corner with the tray.

"This is the lady with nineteen children, Mandy," was Jill's introduction.

Mandy stared.

"Bless you, woman!" was her country greeting. Then she said irrelevantly, "Though we had a sow farrowed fifteen last year—"

Jill gave her a look.

But the woman did not notice.

She was drinking the tea, making loud noises that made Jill set her teeth.

When she had finished she set down the cup, took up a cream biscuit, and said, "You'll never punch me away from here, miss."

Jill burst out laughing.

But the tears were in her eyes, too.

The woman reminded her of a poor ewe that had been worried by its lambs.

"There's a party," said Jill, "this afternoon. But if you'd rather rest, don't come. I'll show you your room." She did.

The mother of nineteen did not attend the party. Through the applause greeting Mrs. Briggs' speech, which began, "I stand here as a mother of eight—" through the clink of the tea-cups, through the speech of an old parson, the laughter of the farmers' wives through all the fun and games, and mutual congratulations of that eventful day—the mother of nineteen slept.

When a "set" was formed, in the flat field at the foot of the Firstlings, she still slept on, though the other two mothers jigged it with the rest. Peggy danced with old Giles, to his great dismay, and Jill found herself footing it with Will Mason.

"Everything has gone off splendidly!" said Jill, with a sigh of relief.

"What were you afraid of?" asked Mason. Five hundred pounds loss and—a big heartache! This was his share in Jill's big day.

"I don't know !" she laughed.

"There'll be difficulties, of course," he said "There always are. But that's part of the game."

He could smell the spikes of lavender in her belt. He was dancing with the only girl in the world for him.

" Didn't Mrs. Briggs speak *beautifully*? asked Jill.

Mason smiled good-humouredly.

" Quite as well as most openers," he said. His moment was passing.

The music of the fiddlers was slackening; the sun was going down—and some few of the guests were only waiting for the dance to be over before departing.

" I must get this train," he said, as he released Jill.

" Oh—must you go ? " she asked.

He nodded.

Then he said, quietly, " If ever you want any advice— you may, you know—people sometimes do—write to me. I'll give it to the best of my ability. Though—I've never been—a mother. The main point you must watch is—the economics. Women never do, and I think you would least of all. It may sound sordid, but, after all, Firstlings' House rests on your remaining thousands. If that goes—it might degenerate into a Charitable Institution, whereas now it is a gift—a beautiful Gift—to Life, and those who pay most heavily for it. Remember, Jill."

He was gone before she could recover, before she could feel that tumult of indignation at his advice, that resentment which said it *was* sordid to speak of the money basis—and then, after all, the realisation that perhaps he was right, and a determination to look after the economics. Oh, Jill! Never was there a Bennett yet who could do that!

She was snapped up by Peggy, who was staying the week-end, and was to take a full report to the committee.

"The mother of nineteen is asking for you," said Peggy.

Jill was yet quivering.'

"If you had nineteen children, Peggy," she said, "you wouldn't laugh."

"It would be the biggest joke in the world," said Peggy. "I should *always* love the teeny-weeniest best. Wouldn't you?"

Then she said, "Oh—forgive me, Jill. I—forgot—"

"Forgot what?" said Jill, hurrying off to the mother of nineteen.

"That you had lost your sweetheart," said Peggy.

"I wish I could," murmured Jill, which made Peggy stare.

CHAPTER VI

JILL BREAKS RULES

"I shall really have to have a secretary!" moaned Jill.

She was sitting on the little chair with the fat, round cushion. At her feet were letters, on the table were letters, and her remark was followed by the click of the letter-box.

Mandy was sitting knitting in the corner of the room. Sunshine fell on her white hair and the old, placid face, with its kind wrinkles.

"More mothers!" she smiled, and picked up a stitch she had let fall.

Jill had asked Mandy into her holy-of-holies room, because Mandy rested her. Jill had a pain just at the nape of the neck, worse than any she had known in the office of the blue gauze blind. She dreamt letters at night—letters and mothers, and domestic confidences and financial problems, and husbands who didn't want "to be left," who wrote Jill unique protests, the worst of which had been anonymous and scurrilous, the best of which had been humorous, but sorrowful!

"Five hundred letters in three days, Mandy," sighed Jill. Then she broke into one of her little quavers of laughter. She was looking through the window.

Outside, in a huge apron that well-nigh swallowed her, the mother of nineteen was actually cleaning the garden steps. As she washed them, a little of her tongue could be seen—in her violent anxiety to do them well—pushed to one side of her mouth.

Jill ran out to the top of the steps.

"Oh, Mrs. Hamer," she said, with mock reproach. "You are going to get the house a bad name!"

Mrs. Hamer looked up.

She was a little less "jumpy" than on her arrival.

Jill hastened to quiet the alarm in her glance. Mrs. Hamer was not a humorist. Perhaps it was too much to expect of a mother of nineteen.

"I mean," smiled Jill, gently, "this is a *Rest* House."

"I'm—restin'," said Mrs. Hamer. "I'm sort o' got up with my sleep, miss."

Jill did not smile now—though all the rest of the House had done so on account of the quality and quantity of the mother of nineteen's slumbers!

For four days and nights it seemed that she had done nothing but want "leaving alone"—and Jill had sent her meals into the bedroom.

But then, Jill knew more about Mrs. Hamer than anyone else in the house. In that little blue room Mrs. Hamer had told her something of the slow breaking down under the strain—until she really had feared she would commit suicide, and, in a mad moment, had asked the police, to take her and put her — safe."

Now there was a tinge of colour in her cheeks. As Jill went away she half-imagined she heard Mrs Hamer humming as she worked at the steps.

So far, Mandy was doing the housekeeping, and each woman turned out her own room.

Jill was determined that she was going to keep Firstlings House on a sound financial basis. The interest from her five thousand pounds was not too much to cover the weekly expenditure. But Jill did not intend to have any subscribers to her scheme. She knew what that would mean.

She had already had letters from social workers, ministers of the Gospel, Literary and Debating Societies and a Professor of Physical Culture—with a note and a couple of handbooks from a Theosophist. Jill had pursed her pretty mouth firmly over each one. Her mothers had come there to *rest*, not to swallow tinpot theories. Therefore—Jill meant to need money from no one for the forwarding of her scheme. But she had sighed over the numerous applications to come.

Had she had five millions it is possible she would have stood a Rest House on every hill in the country. But, even then, Jill knew there would still be something wrong, *very* wrong. And it is a unique social reformer who has the courage to make that admission.

She went back into her little blue room, finding Mandy had gone into the great kitchen to make dinner. Two of the mothers were helping her. One was shelling beans. The other was counting out plates and singing "God be with you till we meet again." Mrs. Briggs, who four days ago had got her name into print, as the opener, was going back on the morrow. Jill had been unable to persuade her to leave the children any longer.

Mrs. Briggs' husband was proud of the newspaper paragraph—but a little dubious as to whether an "opener" should not be paid! At present Mrs. Briggs was reading "Cranford" in her bedroom. For a "mother of eight" who had only read two books in her life before, and those when she was a girl, Mrs. Briggs had a wholesome scent for a good book.

Jill had advised her to sit with her feet up pretty high, for that internal weakness, and Mrs Briggs had adopted a position familiar to her from seeing Mr. Briggs in it, every night, whilst she bathed the family.

But the first time she had sat in that position she had wondered if it was the thing, until Jill assured her that really well-off young ladies sat so, had no internal weakness, who just went to clubs, to talk about books.

"Well, if they can do it!"—said Mrs. Briggs, of Poplar!

Jill could hear all the little sounds from the kitchen and the murmur of the voices of the mothers. Two more were arriving that afternoon. One was from Scotland, the other from a Welsh mining village—and Jill was just thinking how to answer the miner's wife in Northumberland, whose letter was an indictment against the conditions the bearers of the race have to live under. She had four sons, a daughter, and a husband. The five men worked on three different "shifts". Always the big wooden tub was on the fire, ready for the wash of the grimy ones on their return. Always the food was on the table of the dark house. Always the wet clothes, gritty with coal-slack dust, hung round the fire. Always she slept the broken sleep of those who tend on the breadwinners who must have meals for day-shift and night-shift.

Jill did not know how to answer this letter. It was against the Committee's laid-down rules that anyone with more than three pounds a week coming in could come to the House. Jill pondered it. Her bit of Irish blood stirred.

"Come," she wrote back—and enclosed two pounds for the single fare. Oh, Jill! So determined to look after the economics—and always that bit of Bennett coming up. Breaking rules and making exceptions. But she kept to that rule which only sent a woman the single fare, lest she should go home before the "cure" was up.

A month was the least time a woman was supposed to come for—unless a rare exception.

Jill had broken the first rule for her "opener."

Jill wrote steadily for a couple of hours, answering letters wise, foolish, weak, strong, beautiful, and some of them sordid and selfish. Jill had instinct. She guessed just the sort of people behind those letters. Naturally, she wanted the nice mothers. So far she had got them. But now—she wrote to one of the other kind. She had talked it over with Mandy, and Mandy had said, "After all, there's not much credit doing nice things for nice folk, is there?"

Jill had asked a woman to come who swore—actually swore—in her application to come to the Guest House. Jill had guessed that she would lie too—and, possibly, *steal*. A "dangerous" woman, but—poor, beastly poor, with a husband sand-hawking, and three children, one of whom was blind and one ruptured. The only troubling thought to Jill was, "Had she, Jill, a right to ask the nice mothers to meet this one?"

Jill was really a little autocratic. She decided that it might even be good for the others.

But little did she dream the anxiety Martha Smith would cause her. Though had she known it is quite likely she would have done just the same. Jill, who did not stick to cast-iron rules, had a great belief that the best impulses in our hearts cost us less than we should lose by not following them.

That afternoon the mothers were having tea in the garden, all sitting in basket chairs and afterwards Mrs. Briggs was going to read "Cranford" to them— and they were going to talk and laugh about it. There was a little box in the hall into which they could drop suggestions as to how their days should be spent. On the morrow they were going bilberrying on Brown Moss moors, from morning until sunset. That had been Jill's suggestion, dropped into the box along with theirs.

The letter-writing done, Jill leaned back, her eyes half-closed.

From the dining-room came sounds of preparation for dinner. She would just have ten minutes to herself. Her eyes closed slowly. But she was not asleep. Jill was day-dreaming, and the dream had nothing to do with Firstlings House. A little smile played around her lips. The strain of the last few days faded from her brain. Whatever the dream was it was very pleasant.

Its end, however, was almost galvanic. Jill jumped up from her chair with a suddenness that only belonged to Jill, in common with Jack-in-the-boxes, but which in Jill had a gracefulness such sudden movement does not usually have.

"Jill Bennett!" she murmured, in self-disgust.

She dashed a tear from her lashes.

"Dinner, Miss Bennett," said Mrs. Briggs, just on the other side of the door.

"Coming," said Jill, cheerfully.

She tidied herself up, straightening her hair by aid of the dim reflection she could see of herself in the glass of the Rainy Day picture.

Then she opened the door, and passed out to face the mothers, her face radiant as it had grown to be in the happiness that came to her from the mothers.

The "mother of eight," her face expressing shades of both joy and sorrow that she was going home, was carrying in the roast beef. She beamed at Jill. Jill was struck with sadness to think that Mrs. Briggs was going back to buy scraps of poor meat.

She entered the large dining-room. The creamy walls, bright under the sunlight, were cheerful with gay-painted plates, peasant ware. Two long tables were set on the black-and-white tiles of the floor. Sprays of autumn leaves, mountain-ash berries, pots of golden hawksbit and purple scabious were set the length of Irish linen tablecloths. The only ornament or picture in the room was a figure on the white fire-shelf—a statuette of a woman with a child on her right arm, and her left hand carrying a sheaf of wheat.

The mothers sat down, Mandy at the head of the table, Jill at the foot.

There was a little pause, in which Mandy looked beseechingly at Jill, in which Jill looked back at Mandy. Over the knitting the old woman had been expressing herself on the subject of grace before meat. Jill was hot convinced. She was afraid of making the mothers uncomfortable. Jill felt she must die if they should think for one moment that she was bringing them there for any other reason than of giving them a rest.

Then—Mandy bent her capped head.

Mandy had been thinking since she had talked with Jill. She believed a unique grace was wanted at this table.

"May nobody ever have any less, Lord!" said Mandy, in a hushed voice.

Jill suppressed a desire to laugh and scream. She felt that a little thrill ran all along the table, both sides.

They waited for more.

But Mandy lifted up her head, and took up the carving knife.

Jill stole a glance at her mothers, when she dared. They were looking at Mandy in a new way. And, for the first time at dinner, they began to talk—several at once—telling what they *did* have, and had had, and would have again, and of their friends who scrambled to get bread and margarine and a bit of poor jam for the children; and how some of those children drank out of the same pot, and shared the same spoon, and the sort of rooms they ate in, all littered with work, and sometimes dirt—because mothers had to scramble for bread, too.

"They'd think we had gone mad if they see us now," said the mother of nineteen.

Quite suddenly, she gulped.

It was the first touch of unselfish feeling she had shown. Mrs. Hamer had been an automaton on her arrival, and a worn one at that.

She was thinking, for the first time, of the children she had left—left without one pang of conscience; left, running like a mad woman to catch the train that would take her right away, out of the noise and the dirt the muddle.

But when Mandy handed down the table buns with real cream on the top, Mrs. Hamer was herself again.

The mothers went to lie down after dinner. Jill retired to her little blue room. She also was very tired.

CHAPTER VII

MARTHA SMITH

That same afternoon Jill was to meet the train bringing the Welsh mother and Scottish mother.

She was awakened from her short rest by someone tapping on her door, and, opening it sleepily, saw Mrs. Briggs.

"Come in," said Jill.

This was her private room, into which she was allowing everybody to come.

"If it's not taking a liberty," said the mother of eight.

Jill had got very fond of her. Her grey, crisped hair framed a pleasant, homely face with very brown eyes.

Jill smiled.

Mrs. Briggs entered. "I've brought you this," she said.

"This" was a long length of black silk, crewelled with pink rosebuds, blue forget-me-nots, and white jasmine.

"Oh!" gasped Jill.

There were hundreds of hours of patient work in the silk strip.

"I put the forget-me-nots in whilst I was sitting up after my eldest was born," said Mrs. Briggs, with a soft look. "But I never got time after. They came every year—till I put my foot down," she said, with dignity.

Jill and she both stood, the length of silk in their hands between them. Jill felt very near to Mrs. Briggs.

But—she winced at taking it. She knew it was the most beautiful thing in Mrs. Briggs' life, after the children.

She tried to form words to refuse it, graciously, but something held them back.

Mrs. Briggs was looking at her expectantly.

Jill, who was a good giver, was a poor receiver, but something made her chary of what she said in answer to Mrs. Briggs' offer.

"I think," said Jill, her head on one side, like a robin's, "it will just be the thing to border Mandy and me two Sunday aprons."

Joy shone from Mrs. Briggs' face. She drew a deep breath.

"I was afraid," she confessed, "you wouldn't have it, because it was old-fashioned."

And Jill found out the great graciousness there is in receiving a gift.

She ran Mandy an apron up that very afternoon, and put the border on. Then she went off to meet the train that brought the two mothers.

Sitting on the little platform, Jill was thinking of the project that had entered her head since Mason gave her his parting injunction. She was dissatisfied with the interest her money was making. If it made double, that meant she could take twice as many mothers.

Jill, who had never been greedy, was suddenly getting greedy. To get more meant to be able to give more.

She had just decided the question when the train puffed in.

Jill stood watching the people. Her eyes were on a little woman, tinier even than herself. She was not shabbily dressed, but looked so tired Jill expected her to faint on the platform.

Jill was advancing a step towards her, when a voice sounded just behind her. It had almost a masculine depth, and nearly made Jill jump.

"Do ye ken the way to Firstlings' Guest Hoose" it inquired.

Jill stared into the strong, sweet face of the Scottish mother. She was about thirty, no more. The only masculine thing about her was her deep voice and her height.

"I'm Miss Bennett," said Jill.

The Scotch mother made her feel a very bairn.

Then, over her shoulder, Jill saw the small, pathetic figure trailing along, looking dazedly in her direction.

"This is another mother," murmured Jill, and went to meet her.

"Are you Mrs. Williams?" asked Jill.

The Glamorgan woman looked at Jill.

"Let's have tea in the station-house," said Jill.

She did not believe the frail little woman could get to Firstlings. So they had buns and tea in the station-house. Then they went to Firstlings.

As they ascended the hill the laughter and clink of teacups came to them from the garden.

Mrs. Williams went to her room. But the Scottish mother, with her fine staying powers, washed the dust from herself and went forth to the garden.

Jill left Mrs. Williams alone. She took tea alone, too, in her own little room, but went down to the reading of "Cranford." It was funnier than ever, as Mrs. Briggs read it.

£Click!" said the post-box.

Jill left the mothers discussing the merits of "Cranford."

There was a letter in the hand-writing she was looking for. She opened it. It was in Mason's big sprawl. She read with a sense of bewilderment. It was a very brief letter. It did not even begin in the usual way. She read:—

"Do you love me? Yes or no? Can't stand this suspense any longer. You must have known for an eternity.

> Will Mason."

Jill looked at the envelope again. Then she pondered the sentences—"an eternity"—"can't stand this suspense any longer."

The flush died off her cheeks, leaving them pale.

Jill had a quick brain. She thought she guessed what Mason had done.

He had been writing to her about the Guest House, and to Susan at the same time. He had sent the proposal of marriage, which was meant for Susan, to herself. There was no other explanation! She had only known Mason six months. That couldn't be an eternity. He had known Susan all his life.

It was only when she had re-posted the note to Susan, with a short explanation from herself, that doubts assailed her. Anyhow, events would tell.

Three days later Will Mason opened a letter from his Cousin Susan.

He sat back and gasped. The horror of what he had done burst on him. He must have put the letter intended for Jill into the envelope addressed to Susan. And Susan had *jumped at him*—absolutely jumped! She had written a letter confessing she had loved him all her life.

* * * * * *

Mandy noticed that Jill was rather more quiet during the next two days. But after Mandy mentioned it she obviously strove to be less preoccupied.

"And I thought she was getting over it nicely!" sighed Mandy to Giles, thinking Jill was still mourning the "burying of him".

Despite herself, Jill ran whenever the letter box clicked.

It was four days before a letter arrived with the Devon postmark. Jill tore it open with an eagerness of which she felt ashamed. When she read it Jill was suddenly conscious of just how eager she had been to hear from Susan James.

The light died out of her face as she read. She told herself that she had known all the time. Susan was full of gratitude that Jill had sent "her letter" on. She had been expecting this letter from her cousin. She would write again.

She did—three days after that. The letter arrived on Sunday. Jill read it in her little room.

Susan James was formally engaged to her cousin, she told Jill.

With a forlorn feeling Jill turned to her work. She didn't admit it was for solace—solace for a hurt that was certainly not connected with the "burying of him."

As it happened, she had her hands full. After writing congratulations back to Susan (Susan sent the letter to Mason, who groaned), Jill put the whole foolish episode out of her mind. Mason was not the only one with a will!

Martha Smith arrived on the Monday.

Jill, looking out of the little blue-room window, engrossed with housekeeping accounts, observed a hard-faced, black-eyed woman standing looking up at the house. Down at heel, yet showily dressed, she had a slightly aggressive expression. She held by the hand a girl-child of eight, with a seeking expression of countenance that told she was blind.

Jill's quick sympathy stirred, together with a wild feeling against the woman, who, despite money sent expressly to get someone to attend to her children whilst she was away, had brought the girl in defiance of the rules Jill had forwarded.

"Mrs. Smith?" queried Jill from the top, of the steps.

"Yes, ma'am," said Martha Smith.

The deference of her tone was contradicted by the boldness of her look.

"*Something* made her like that," thought Jill. "Well, it can't be helped."

Aloud, she only said, kindly, "Come in Mrs. Smith. You must be very tired."

She said nothing with reference to the little girl. Martha Smith set Jill down as an utter "softy."

"Twelve steps, Beatrice," she told the little girl. Jill started.

"Beatrice" was the name of her own twin sister, asleep in that grave that held her father. She had died at the age of this poor child of the clumsy boots and bedraggled look.

She gave them tea with her own hands, for she had made Mandy lie down because she had complained of pains in her feet.

Mandy's brother had not been well, and she had had a lot of running about.

The "mother of nineteen" assisted by the Scottish mother, was making tea for the rest that afternoon. Janet Burns had baked the scones and Mrs. Hamer had made the ice-buns. The buzz of their voices came to Jill as she sat watching little Beatrice Smith grope hungrily for the cake.

Then when they were rested Jill said, watching Martha Smith, "Of course, Mrs. Smith, it is a rule of Firstlings that no mother brings her family with her. You read the rules, I suppose?"

And because she was so young, so much luckier than they were, so conscious that she had scarcely the right to add any reproach to their bedraggled lives, much as they left to be desired, Jill blushed as she spoke, and felt shame in her heart, as though she had been the Pharisee she was *not*.

Martha stammered apologies that were lies. Jill knew they were lies.

Little Beatrice had a crushed, shamed expression on her face. It was an old face for a child of eight—the sort of face that said she knew, little as she was, that cocoa and milk were too dear for little folk in her position. Jill felt a lump in her throat.

"I shall send the child into the village,' she said. "You know, Mrs. Smith, if we allowed *one* child, it would mean more. The house is for the mothers' rest. So I must explain to the others *that you did not quite understand*".

Jill's soft brown eyes looked straight into the beady black ones of Martha Smith. Martha received a little shock. Her gaze wavered before Jill's—the young, soft, pretty thing in the apple-green dress.

"Yes, ma'am," she said, with the humility that was more awful to Jill than her boldness!

"The others are going into the garden,' said Jill. "Come along, Beatrice." She took the child by the hand and they departed, leaving Martha to wash, and find the others.

She left the child, a guest, at an old farmhouse, playing with other children, who said they would take care of her. Jill knew that the farmer's wife would love and feed her, for she had a heart big enough to hold the world.

CHAPTER VIII

JILL'S FAMILY BRINGS TROUBLE

WHEN Jill got back from arranging for Beatrice at the farmhouse, she found Martha Smith had introduced herself to everybody. Martha was quite satisfied with herself, and Jill guessed, from her face, and the looks of the others, that she was telling them the trick she had played in bringing the blind child with her. When Jill met them all at supper, she saw quite plainly that the mother who was not "nice" had brought the apple of discord in her hand.

The battle between Jill and the sand-hawker's wife began—silently, but grimly.

Jill's troubles that week were legion.

Giles fell and hurt his arm. Mandy had to return home to see to him. The post of housekeeper was filled each day by one of the mothers. But the plan was not a success. Out of the dozen mothers at Firstlings only six were decent cooks. After all, they had not had the stuff that inspires and stimulates in the culinary arts. Every day, Jill went down to see if Giles's arm was better. But as Mandy said, "his bones were like chalk, and this would be a long do."

On the top of the housekeeping muddle, Jill was worried about Mrs. Hamer.

The "mother of nineteen" had become depressed since Martha Smith arrived. They talked in corners together. Jill pretended to ignore the evident conspiracy.

She was not surprised when Mrs. Hamer tapped on her door one afternoon when she was trying to rest.

Jill had now entirely abandoned the idea of having this as a private room.

"Come in!" she sang out.

Mrs. Hamer came in with a guilty look. Physically she was not the same woman. Jill had made her a dress, too, by aid of Janet Burns, and one of the mothers had been experimenting on her hair. The "mother of nineteen" wavered a little when she saw Jill smiling at her, like an angel, in an apple-green dress.

But she made the straight attack.

"Please, Miss Bennett," she said, "I want to go home."

Jill, three days before, had written an enchanting letter to Mr. Hamer—enclosing a five-pound note for him to get someone in for two weeks to look after him. That morning came his letter of thanks. He had got someone, and he hoped Lizzie was better.

"Why?" asked Jill, looking at Mrs. Hamer in surprise.

"I'm 'omesick," answered Elizabeth Hamer. She looked at Jill, tears in her eyes.

"You know," said Jill, "it's not worth that long journey if you don't stay the time out."

"I seen a little boy—with hair the colour of my Jimmy's," said Mrs. Hamer. Her voice was hysterical.

Jill felt herself weakening. Then she turned sharply on Mrs. Hamer.

"This is Martha Smith's work," she said with that autocratic spurt that was so contradictory to her real normal self.

Jill was feeling angry at herself for all the "exceptions" she had made. And when Mrs. Hamer could not deny that Martha and she had "talked," Jill's mind was made up.

"You must stay the month out," said Jill. "I can't let you go back before you are cured. Do you know, Mrs. Hamer, that when you came here you were qualifying for a brain disease?"

She looked very like her father, when he laid down the law to a patient, as she said this.

"I'm better now," said Mrs. Hamer, feebly!

But Jill's Irish blood was up. Nothing would move her. She wanted to make a perfect cure of Elizabeth Hamer.

Jill missed Mandy very much. There did not seem anyone to turn to. All the mothers were older than she.

The Northumberland mother arrived the next day. She was a large, cheerful woman with a round laugh arid a philosophic outlook, and brought her crocheting out an hour after her arrival. That night the mothers were improvising a go-as-you-please concert. Jill had promised to sing, and two fiddlers were coming up from the village.

Jill never forgot that evening.

The concert was held in the drawing-room.

The great beaded lamps were lit, and the fire was roaring in the wide chimney.

Janet Burns sang "Bonnie Mary of Argyle " in that deep voice like a man's, and after the applause got up and told how she had once won a prize at a singing competition, though everyone had laughed at her.

"I think," said the Scottish mother, smilelessly, "it was my feet got me the prize."

Whereupon there was a burst of laughter.

Everybody did their bit. It was the funniest, most varied, unexpected sort of programme in the world.

When Jill sang one of Grieg's Cradle Songs there was absolute silence after; then she *must* sing again.

So she sang "Winken, Blinken, and Nod," which made some of the mothers cry—in a pleased way. Mandy had come up for an hour, in her silk dress which she only wore about every two years. As for the fiddlers, they played reels, hornpipes, barn-dances, and old tunes to the delight of everyone, and in the pause was heard the voice of the little Welsh mother, saying she never, never should forget the time she was having if she lived to be a thousand, which Jill thought sadly was not likely. For the Welsh mother had a weak heart.

When she sang in Welsh, it was the star item on the long programme. Nobody knew what it was about, except that it was beautiful. Though when she had finished she was quite exhausted. Mandy came round with the cake stand and glasses of milk. It was then that Jill discovered that the "mother of nineteen" had slipped away.

Some foreboding made her tap at Mrs. Hamer's door. There was no answer.

Jill went into the room. There was a note on the table. It was very brief: "I'ave gon back," it said.

Jill went running about the lanes. Mrs. Hamer had no return ticket, and only ten shillings. There was no train to London that night. No woman answering her description had booked anywhere.

Jill did not sleep that night. Just after breakfast she received a wire. It came from Bingley, and stated that Mrs. Hamer could walk no further. Jill caught the ten train to Bingley, and went to the cottage that had been given as Mrs. Hamer's address. She found her sitting weeping by the fire.

Jill had been thinking hard all the night.

"Do you want to go back *very* much?" she asked, softly.

Whereupon Mrs. Hamer sobbed harder than ever, vowing she would have walked all night again if her legs had not given way. She looked it, too. There was a grim determination, for all her tears, to get to those children who had made her half-crazy—or to die.

"I think," said Jill humorously, "you are a perfect cure, Mrs. Hamer."

Mrs. Hamer went off in the train for London. It could not go fast enough. And Jill reported to headquarters why Mrs. Hamer had gone.

That night Jill went into the kitchen to make supper. When she reached the doorway she heard her own name. Martha Smith was in the centre of a group of the women.

"She's a bleeding tyrant!" Martha said, "and before I go I shall tell her myself. Didn't she get her money out of you an' me, and the likes of us?—"

"No," said Jill, coolly, from the doorway. "Unless any of you ever worked in sugarcanes out where the negroes are? Did you ever make sugar, Mrs. Smith?"

If a bomb had dropped Martha could not have been more surprised.

"I am waiting," said Jill, "to hear you tell me about myself."

But Martha Smith's fire had died away. The women filed out of the kitchen. Jill sat down on the stool in the corner by the oven.

Martha waited, wondering if she would be told to quit.

"Mis. Smith," said Jill, "have you anything to say against me? Criticism will be welcome."

Martha's colour paled. She had expected being told what she owed Jill. She merely shook her head.

"There is more on my plate, at present, than I can manage," Jill went on, "So you can consider yourself, during your stay here, as housekeeper and cook. I shall, of course, pay you good wages."

Martha's mouth opened and closed.

Jill apparently did not see her astonishment,, but got up, and showed her where everything was.

"Supper at nine," said Jill, and walked away, leaving Martha in a stunned condition.

But when she brought-supper in she did it with an air that said there was nothing like standing up to folk to get a post of honour.

Jill knew that she must now look out for a series of petty deceptions and dishonesties. She was not wrong.

Martha set out to rob Jill at all ends and turns. Jill let her go on, until she caught her in the act of sending off teaspoons home.

"Haven't those spoons turned up?" asked Jill, innocently.

Martha shook her head.

"Somebody must have pinched 'em!" she said, indignantly. Jill looked at her.

"Oh, no," she said.

"Well, where can they have gone to?" asked Martha.

Jill's glance had never moved from her face.

"They are here," said Jill, and shook a box, addressed to Mr. Smith, and parcelled.

Shame appeared on Mrs. Smith's face.

"Are you short of spoons at home?" asked Jill, with the same straight look.

Mrs. Smith did not answer.

"Because, if you are, you can have them," said Jill, gently. "Those are very good spoons. But I'm sure the six apostles left behind will be sorry to part from the other six. So do you mind taking them all?"

"What I believe is—she's mad," said Mrs. Smith, to the others, afterwards, without telling them why.

But she began to see Jill in a new light. Every day something disappeared. Every day Jill found it out, and gave Mrs. Smith something else. But Mrs. Smith did not soon give way under "coals of fire." In fact, she seemed pretty asbestic!

It was when Mrs. Smith stole a pair of gloves from the Scottish woman that Jill grew stem. She spoke to Mrs. Smith in the trenchant manner that Harry Thorn had quailed under. But somehow or other she managed to keep the Scottish woman's faith that they had been "lost."

And—Martha Smith began to feel uncomfortable at Firstlings. She hated Jill more than anyone she had ever met, because Jill gave her so many chances, and—understood: her so well.

The last straw was when Jill made little Beatrice a silk dress.

Martha broke out into a torrent of abuse, called Jill a Pharisee, asked Jill if she had not prayed for her, cursed Firstlings from floor to roof, said she was going home, and burst into tears—human tears— murmuring between them that she was as good as they made them—without paint; as good as Jill; as good as anyone there; nay, better.

Jill stood listening. Her eyes were very bright.

"You silly mother!" she said. "I have never thought you a sinner."

"Nor prayed for me?" gasped Martha Smith.

Jill shook her head.

"It never entered my head," she said. "I—I never pray myself. But—Mandy prays for me."

"For *you!*" said Martha faintly.

"H'm!" acknowledged Jill, without scorn.

"An', ain't you mad?" asked Martha.

Jill shook her head.

"Then—what?" stammered Martha.

"You poor thing!" said Jill, giving Martha a hearty English kiss. "If I had been in your place, I think I should have been the most wicked woman in the world!"

Martha stared.

Then—she opened her heart, and her mouth. She told the truth. From the earliest she could remember she had lived a life of hell. She had been up for stealing old stockings, bits of oilcloth, buns, and umbrellas. The first time it had been *bread* she had stolen. She got a month, at the age of nineteen, when Beatrice was a baby.

Jill sat and grieved with her over the misery she had endured, without pointing out the faults.

Two days later Jill missed two notes. She found them unexpectedly next morning, And after that—fact is sometimes stranger than fiction—Jill never missed so much as a pin.

CHAPTER IX

HARRY THORN TURNS UP

NOW that the mothers were pretty settled, Jill began to long to run up to London. Leaving Martha as housekeeper, Janet Burns, with her shrewd head, as guardian, to receive the mothers who came, Jill set out, taking the frail little Welsh Woman with her.

Of all the mothers Jill liked Mrs. Williams best. She was nearest Jill's own age. Her life had been "interesting." The little brown-eyed woman had even been a lay-preacher. Jill could imagine her preaching in Welsh—the frail body lit up by the tense little soul. She could also imagine the drunken father, carrying a child through a field of corn, on a moonlight night, and falling, and the tiny child believing they were going down a hole into hell. Jill felt very humble.

Beside this woman's childhood, her own had been a paradise. For the outlay of her ten thousand she was getting big interest—the biggest interest in the world, in fact—contact with other lives, their memories, joys, sorrows, hopes and fears. Twenty times a day Jill told herself that, however the scheme worked out, she had already more than got her money's worth.

Mrs. Williams, having luncheon with Jill in the dining-car, looked at her dreamily.

"It is," she said, out of her dream, "some young man you are going to see?"

They had the dining-car to themselves.

"Oh—no!" said Jill, simply and directly. But she flushed and whitened. She could not feel angry with

Mrs. Williams. What would have been rudeness in some of the other mothers was distinction in her.

Jill noticed that, despite the poor fare she was accustomed to, she did not seem delighted with the dining-car set out. As a matter of fact, Mrs. Williams ate without worrying about food at all, just as fine folk who can have what they like until they never think about it. Jill admired her more and more.

But she felt some explanation was due as to their errand, and in a half-hysterical moment, which arose from the consciousness that she was giving herself away, she said: "Well—you see, Mrs. Williams—I buried him."

Mrs. Williams nodded.

"You are going to see his grave," she concluded, softly. Her brown eyes filled with tears. Jill was surprised. The most penetrating of the mothers, Mrs. Williams had struck Jill as a little hard.

When they had settled themselves in their seats, jolting along through Derbyshire, which was one blaze of October gold, Jill said, looking from behind the *Delineator*, "Mrs. Williams, if ever I cease to be house-mother at Firstlings, I shall install you in my stead."

Mrs. Williams laughed at the bare idea of such a thing.

When they got out of the train Mrs. Williams was impressed. It had been the dream of her life to see London. But for Jill she would have gone out of London a corpse "many a time over," as Jill said, with her flash of absurd Irishisms that had used to make Thorn laugh. The Celtic dreamer from the mountainland saw London through wonderful spectacles.

"I love them," she said, suddenly, to Jill.

Jill got her on a little island.

"Love whom?" she asked.

"People!" said Mrs. Williams.

She was watching them go by, hearing their feet, the endless procession of them, hearing the murmur of their voices, seeing their faces. She would have stood there hours, had Jill allowed it. But Jill got a taxi, and they went to the Chambers; at the same time she realised again that in case anything did happen that would call her from Firstlings, Mrs. Williams was the woman to take her place. In fact, Jill felt a little humble beside the frail woman who could only bear dead babies, and who loved *people,* people, people, with a passionate adoration for the miserable "forked radishes". It was really her instinct to "mother" the World.

It was just as Jill was unlocking the door of her uncle's old room that she heard someone come whistling up the staircase. She kept a stately back, and wrestled valiantly with the key.

Will Mason had to pass that door to climb the flight to his own rooms.

He saw the little Welshwoman sitting on a portmanteau at the side of Jill's door, and dreamily waiting until it was opened, and guessed that this was Jill, wriggling away as she always wriggled at that door, which always opened quite easily.

"Back again? "he said, lightly.

His heart was beating a mad tattoo against his ribs.

Jill lifted her face.

It looked pale, and a little worried.

"Let me open the door," he said.

He did.

"Oh, won't you come in a minute?" asked Jill. "Come in, Mary!"

The little Welshwoman hauled in the bags.

"My friend, Mary Williams," said Jill.

Mason and Mrs. Williams shook hands.

"Won't you stay to tea?" asked Jill.

She was even paler, but her eyes were serene.

Mason accepted the invitation.

He did not even tell himself that he ought not to have done so. Quite by accident he had discovered that after all he could not possibly have put his proposal into an envelope addressed to Susan, for he had found the envelope addressed to Susan, including the cousinly letter. He had forgotten to post it.

Whilst he did not suspect his cousin of any trick, he wanted to know how she had managed to accept his proposal, since he had sent it to Jill.

That will of his that had infuriated the lion was in good working order. He and Susan had it in full, as the Mason inheritance. But being a man convention allowed him to make straight tracks for things—whilst Susan—Susan was treading the labyrinthine paths of the wily feminine after her own way.

They had tea.

"Cupid Brand" peaches!—with the same obese little Cupids sitting on the plump yellow peaches, outside the tin.

Never, never had Mason seen anyone empty peaches into a glass dish as Jill did. He knew it was foolish to think so, even as he thought it. But at the same time he knew he should always think it. He had loved her from the moment he had seen her draw that rough sketch of the Dream House, her face lit up, speaking in every line and expression of her sensible foolish, but always beautiful Mother Heart, whilst she was scarcely more than a child in years.

After tea Mrs. Williams went into the little room to wash up the things. Then, she said she wanted to go out, just to stand and watch the people.

"I'll go with you," said Jill, hurriedly.

"I want to go alone," said Jill's friend.

Her look was emphatic.

"You—you won't come home on a shutter?" said Jill, anxiously.

Mary Williams laughed.

"I'm just going to find a safe place to stand and dream in," she said. "Then—when I wake up—I'll come on here with my eyes open. I *do* have lucid intervals."

Which made both Jill and Mason laugh, and quite took away Jill's fears.

As Mason said good afternoon to Mrs. Williams, and went off before she did, Jill lost that other fear. For Jill was quite determined—quite—that she was not going to have Susan's young man hanging around her.

She was lying back in her chair, thinking she would go to see Mr. Wicks to-morrow, as she felt absurdly tired, when Mason's voice made her start.

"May I come in?" it asked.

He was in the room with the last word.

His plain face looked plainly across at her. Jill had sat up, stiffly, in her uncle's chair—the very chair in which he had written the will which he hoped would bring these two together.

"It isn't much good asking," she said laughing ruefully.

She had made the words as rude as they could be, in defiance of her instinct not to be so.

'* Well—no," smiled Mason, taking the other chair. "But—it's really a point of business I called on."

"Oh!" said Jill.

He smiled at the unconscious clearing of her brow.

They were going to come to grips.

Even under his agitation he knew he should enjoy it. For there was something in his regard for Jill that steadied that agitation. Agitation he had felt before. He had felt it once for Susan. But never mixed with this quiet realisation that of all the girls in the wide world Jill alone could give him that help in life which even men with wills that make lions roar sometimes feel they need.

Even whilst Jill was relieved that he had only called in on a point of business, he dropped his bolt.

"Why did you send that proposal of marriage I sent you on to my cousin?" he asked.

Jill's brown eyes stared dazedly at him out of a blanched face.

She opened her mouth to speak.

Her brain worked rapidly, as it always did at a time of crisis. It worked with that brilliance of rapidity that has given the Irish nation its pre-eminence where brilliance of intellect tells, though it has not the stodgy virtues. How her father would have loved to see his child of the "dilated heart" at this moment, had he been alive!

"I sent it—because I knew you had made a mistake," she said.

"You mean—" he began.

"I mean—I knew you meant it for Susan," she said.

"If—if you had known I had meant it for you," said the strong-willed one.

Like the lion, Jill began to resent.

"Did you really?" she asked, wide-eyed.

Only her pallor showed that she was moved at all.

"For no one else in the world, Jill," said Mason. "Look what a hole you've put me in!"

He did not move an inch nearer to her. He was splendid. Jill knew it.

But—the situation was impossible.

Jill told herself he had got to have Susan now.

While Mason told himself that Jill was his. At least—he was going to run her down, and—tame her, the pride of her. But it is not every man who puts it so plainly to himself.

"But—I—I buried him!" said Jill, flushing.

"Well, he's done with, then," said Mason. "Poor fellow. But I'm not afraid of dead men."

"I—shall never—love again," said Jill.

"I should like," said Mason, lazily, "to see his resting-place."

Jill's brilliance had given out.

"Do you mean that you don't think he's dead?" she asked, sternly.

"Only a very small percentage of people are buried alive," said Mason. "Anyhow, he's dead now—if he *wasn't* dead then—that is, if he was buried."

Jill's frightened eyes looked at him.

Footsteps were coming up the stairs.

Even as they came she told herself it could not be true, that it could not, that nothing so awful could be true, that her brain was playing her a trick.

A knock came to the door.

"Come in," said Jill, with stiff, white lips. Harry Thorn came into the room.

"Oh, pardon me—good night, Miss Bennett," said Mason.

He had lost his head now. He remembered when his feet touched the little green mat, that he had said "good night" at four in the afternoon. He had recognised Thorn as the young man of the miniature.

CHAPTER X

JILL PROPOSES TO HARRY THORN

Harry Thorn stood looking at Jill. She had risen from her chair.

There was a brief silence—that was brief to Jill, but long to Thorn. The man was the first to speak.

"Are you—engaged to that fellow who went out?" he asked, moodily.

"That fellow who went out was a man," said Jill, pointedly.

She could scarcely realise that just over six months ago she had worshipped this individual. Jill was beginning to fear that she had a fickle nature—which was funnier than she guessed. "But—"

"No. I'm not engaged," Jill told him. He heaved a sigh of relief.

"I'm—free—too," he said, a little awkwardly.

"What, again?" quoth Jill.

He winced. Then he came across the room to her.

"Look here, Jill," he said, in a low, embarrassed voice, "I'm not quite so mean as you've thought me. You don't know, either, how I hated that office life. That seemed the only way. But I must have been mad to have weighed even freedom against—you."

He looked at her appealingly.

"How did you find out where I lived?" asked Jill, thoughtfully.

"Mrs. Greenwall," he said.

"How did you get *free?*" asked Jill.

She had gone over to the window that looked down on the quiet square, with its dancing shadows of leaves weaving a pattern on the walls.

She missed seeing Thorn wince again at the word "free."

"Miss Wheeler is dead," said Harry, gravely.

Jill burst out laughing. She could not help it. Whilst Harry's horrified face—the shock his decorum had sustained—made her want to laugh more. She knew it was awful to want to laugh at the poor thing being dead—but to think that she had buried Harry, and that he had buried Miss Wheeler!

"You—you are quite sure she's dead, Harry? "asked Jill, struggling with her Irish.

"Quite!" he said.

He was looking at Jill with a half-fear that she was going mad.

"Was it—sudden?" asked Jill.

Her voice was getting respectfully condolent at last. Harry nodded.

"Appendicitis, wasn't it?" asked Jill.

"Yes," he said; then, quickly, "Why—how did you know?"

"Oh, a little bird told me," said Jill, knowingly.

She was struggling with her laughter again; it nearly choked her. To think that appendicitis was the complaint she had chosen for Harry, and—that Sarah Wheeler had died of it!

Harry Thorn saw the first ray of hope since he had entered the room. Jill had been sufficiently interested in his affairs to make inquiries about them, he thought.

He told her something of what had happened to him since their estrangement—the outward and the inward changes. Now, as Jill saw and listened to him, after the first shock of his reappearance was over, she realised that Harry was changed, and for the better; that the terrible mean streak had worked itself out. She realised that he was now on the winning side of fortune—set up in a business suited to his undoubted abilities, and—that he was offering himself again, humbly—very, very humbly, with shame in his heart for that episode in which he had barely realised himself.

"I couldn't do it, Harry," she said, simply.

He did not speak, only looked at her.

"I couldn't," said Jill. "You see—I've buried you."

She told him the whole story—save that she left out the fact that she was in love with Will Mason. Once or twice he was about to interrupt. Jill shook her head at him.

"Don't stop me," she asked, once. "Perhaps I couldn't begin again. That man who went out here saw your photograph once," she said, "and I'd told him you were dead, too. It's so awkward. But, Harry, I'd bury you ten times over before anyone should know I'd been *jilted*—and—jilted as I was jilted. I never knew how proud I was until then. So—what am I to do?"

"Marry me!" begged the young man.

"You are dead," said Jill, emphatically, "I can't marry a dead man."

As she spoke he felt that it was indeed all over.

Jill stood looking at him. Her brows were puckered. Then—they straightened out. A dimple appeared—the odd dimple that showed at the left side of her mouth.

"If," said Jill, doubtfully, "you are very, very sorry for having put me into the position of having to bury you—if you want to do a very gracious thing—be your twin brother, and we'll pretend to be engaged."

Harry Thorn gasped.

"I have a reason," said Jill, "for wanting very, very much, to be engaged for a few months. Will you, Harry?"

She did not look at him as she spoke. He noticed that.

"Tell me all about it, then," he asked. Jill hesitated. She ran her gaze well over him before she decided to trust him. Then, without reservation, she told him all.

"You think," he said, "that he will—"

"He will marry Susan,' said Jill, determinedly. "I'm not having anyone jilted for me."

In that moment Thorn realised the titanic pride of the slim Jill. Moreover, it opened, very slightly, the door of hope for himself. He believed he could win her round again.

"I'll do anything you wish," he said, earnestly.

"You'll—you'll be your brother," said Jill. They fixed everything up, down to the smallest detail.

"If I had only a picture of your grave! "sighed Jill. "You see—his faith that you are dead is a little shaken."

They sat and talked quite a long time.

"If—if Mr. Mason comes—calls before you go," said Jill, "you could kiss me—just to convince him that we are very delirious."

The queenly way in which she said it ought to have convinced Thorn that he would never be exhumed again. But his conceit was as great as Jill's pride. It was badly wounded, but still vital.

In his room Will Mason was pacing the floor. The two great questions that throbbed in his brain were: Why had Jill given this man out to be dead? Why had he himself not written "Dear Jill" before that proposal of his?

He went down the stairs, at length. He wanted to walk, which meant, with him, to think.

"He's coming, Harry!" said Jill, in a panic as they heard his step. The steps came nearer.

"Just there!" directed Jill, showing Thorn where he might kiss her.

The door was half-open.

Jill screwed her face up with a little expression of tolerance that made Thorn feel wild. But he had determined to eat humble pie. As Mason passed the door the echo of a hearty kiss came from that room, and he had a flying picture of Jill, with Thorn's arm round her, and the sound of her startled "Oh!" followed him out. He waited at the foot of the stairs lest she should call for help. Quite melodramatic explanations of this thing flashed through his mind. But, after standing on the mat for two minutes, without moving—to the astonishment of the Devonian caretaker—he opened the door and went out into the street.

"Go away, now," said Jill. Thorn went.

When Mrs. Williams came in she found Jill had a bad headache, which explained to some extent, the look in her eyes. She put Jill to bed.

Next morning Jill went to Mr. Wicks's office. She wanted to re-in vest the money at a greater interest, so that she could have more mothers at Firstlings. They talked the matter over, and it was decided that it would be quite safe to invest the money with a certain county council that wanted to make improvements. The transaction was left in Mr. Wicks's hands.

That afternoon Jill and Mrs. Williams took tea with Mrs. Wicks. And Mr. Wicks said, as he saw them from the garden gate, "My dear Miss Bennett, Mrs. Wicks has got a great fondness for you." Jill smiled in surprise. It was quite true. Mrs. Wicks had made up her mind that Jill was "harmless."

Jill only saw Mason once before her return to Breezeton. Mrs. Williams was out, doing the picture galleries. Jill had gone for a bus-ride. It was just that hour when blue dusk begins to run through the streets, and St. Paul's looks black against a golden sky.

Jill was sitting staring in front of her, down the shining road that the lights were reflected in. She was the only occupant of the top of the bus. A man came and dropped into a seat near her. Jill went on thinking.

"Jill!" she heard, suddenly.

It was Mason.

"Oh—halloa!" said Jill without looking startled.

He came and sat beside her. They did an immense lot of talking. Really, it seemed as though they were afraid to stop. Then he said, "Susan is coming up."

"Oh," said Jill.

There was a silence, in which the conductor could be heard arguing about the payment of a fare downstairs.

Jill screwed up her courage. She looked at Mason with a well-assumed shyness.

"You remember the young man who called?" she began. Mason nodded, His face said he could not forget.

"We are engaged," said Jill, frankly. "He is Mr. Thorn's dead brother—I mean—he is my dead sweetheart's brother—his twin brother—they were very much alike."

"Very much," he answered.

"They tied their sleeves up with different a coloured ribbon, when they were babies, to identify them," said Jill, earnestly.

Mason was not interested.

They discussed Firstlings, by way of a change, It was just as Jill was telling of her triumph over Martha

Smith that they became conscious of a horrible jerk. The bus had skidded!

The next moment Jill was hurled upon Mason, who clutched her.

"It's all right, now," said Jill, extracting herself from his embrace.

It was. But it had been a narrow shave. Mason did not look at Jill. He was too much disturbed. He therefore missed seeing that Jill took three short looks at him.

Mrs. Williams arrived on the mat just as they did.

I've been out looking for you," she said to Jill.

Jill smiled.

Mrs. Williams would not realise that London was more than a magnified village. She had tickled Jill, too, by thinking she saw people from home in every thoroughfare. A Miss James has called," said Mrs. Williams. "She says she stayed here before."

CHAPTER XI

MANDY IS DEAD

Susan had arrived. There was no help for it; Jill had to ask Mason to supper.

They went out and found Susan, a cool, rested, very joyous Susan, who offered her cheek to her cousin in a way that said she unmistakably believed he *had* meant the proposal for her, or else she was the most determined woman in the world.

He kissed her. It was a very wooden sort of kiss.

Jill's hand shook as she poured out the tea. Susan, flushed and radiant, was such a picture that she convinced Jill that Mason,,would marry her—would care for her, if he did not now.

Susan was full of news from the little Devon village, and from Will's mother. She was staying a week, which meant that Jill must stay longer than she had wanted to, to play hostess. It was a terrible week to Jill.

Susan and Mason, Mason and Susan—they filled her mind. She dreamed of them at night.

If only she was back amongst the mothers!

That was always the hysterical cry of her heart. She learned the difference now between the shock she had sustained at the hands of Harry Thorn, and the hurt she got from seeing Susan and Mason together. There were moments when she felt like pouring her heart out to Mrs. Williams. The ache got to feel more than she could bear. Then she thought of Mandy, and was comforted.

What a relief came when she saw Susan pack up, to know that she could go back to Firstlings and Mandy next day.

Susan was going by the night train. Jill made the old trifle that she had made on the night of the dance that never came off.

She was the only one who would not touch it, saying "No"—almost fiercely.

It was greatly praised.

A telegram arrived for Jill—brought up by the caretaker.

She read it at the door; listening to the coughing of the old man as he went down the stairs. Then she walked back into the room, quite dumb, the orange telegram in her hand, looking at Susan and Mason and Mary Williams, and Harry Thorn (She had asked him to introduce himself to Susan) like one in a dream.

It was Mason who made an involuntary movement towards Jill.

Thorn was quicker than he was. Jill stared at him as though she did not see him.

"This—this is for laughing about Miss Wheeler!" She said; stumblingly.

The streak from the land that has banshees and fairies came uppermost in Jill in this unutterable grief that had fallen upon her.

She sat down, still dizzy.

Then Thorn had picked up the rumpled telegram.

He read it out. It sounded idiotic:—

Monday died Wednesday. Burying Saturday at three.—Janet Burns.

"Mandy! Dear old Mandy!" exclaimed Mason, in a shocked voice.

He had realised the telegraphist's mistake.

Jill got up. She went like a whirlwind towards the door.

She went through another door, without noticing that she did so. She was in her uncle's den. Mason's sympathy had smashed down her control. A heartbroken child that had lost Mandy, she was sobbing great sobs, which she knew could be heard in that other room where people were sitting. The shame that had caused her to flee from the others when she felt her control going was forgotten under this tide of grief that swept over her. She was lying face down on the floor—sobbing as no young woman all English would sob *She had lost Mandy.*

At length she lay quite still.

Automatically the sobs had ceased.

"Jill!" said a low voice at the door. "Open the door."

Jill lay quite spent. She was too weak to lift a finger.

The door knob turned. The door opened.

She jumped, suddenly, into a sitting position.

Mason never forgot her as he saw her then, her face blurred out of recognition almost—her brow puckered, her chin trying to keep still, her hair tossed about her, and—the shame coming back to her, English shame at having given way. She looked almost defiantly at him, to see what he thought of her. His face showed nothing—not even compassion. It was a little paler, that was all. He leaned against the door post, watch in hand.

"You will have to hurry, Miss Bennett," he said, "if you want to catch the train."

He spoke so that those in the other room could hear him.

Then he went away.

Jill came to the sight of the others ten minutes later. She was washed, dressed for travelling, and—English.

Harry Thorn looked a little worried and embarrassed. He was comparing Jill with Susan, thinking how Susan would have acted, under the same circumstances, greatly to Jill's disadvantage.

It was Mason who snatched at Jill's luggage, and carried her cloak, and said he would get her there in time, almost defiantly.

Mrs. Williams, Jill, and Mason got into a taxi, and went off.

Susan and Thorn watched them from the door, with the old caretaker.

"Jill," said Thorn to his companion, "is very warm-hearted, and undisciplined. She's a little Irish, Miss James. Did you kniow?" It was a sort of apology.

"Is she?" asked Susan, with vivid interest.

"Well, that explains it, then!"

She did not say what it explained.

But Susan had remembered that a long time back one of her cousin's maternal ancestors had been Irish. That was why Mason had understood.

Anyhow, that was why Susan liked to explain to herself why he had understood.

* * * * * *

Jill carried with her the recollection of Will Mason's face, with its look that somehow did her good, all through the nightmare of that railway journey—a journey, alas! so different from that other she had taken, to see Mandy, accompanied by him.

That journey seemed a hundred years ago, divided from this one. So much had happened since then. The House for Mothers had then been a dream. Now it was a fact, with the thousand worries that facts and real responsibilities bring.

Then, she had possessed the illusion that she had loved Harry Thorn; that it was her affections, not her pride, he had hurt, when he jilted her. Now she knew that she never had cared for Harry, excepting because he was something to hang on to in the lonely world of London.

Jill found, in dull and pained astonishment, that when she had made up her mind that she had tumbled upon the world's maximum of pain, she had really been only a foolish girl; on the threshold of life, suffering from a shock of pride.

Since then she had made that awful mistake about Mason. And—Mandy was dead.

She couldn't quite realise it yet.

Old people did die, she knew.

Mandy was "getting on."

But she could not quite believe that she would never see Mandy knitting again, Or pottering about making bakes and pies, or talking to Jill about Jill's twin sister, Beatty, and Jill's father—and Jill's mother.

At Crewe, where the fat woman with the baby had got in, and Jill had held the baby whilst the mother had found her ticket, Jill managed to eat a biscuit, just to please Mrs. Williams.

That was early in the morning.

Susan, she knew, would be on her way back to Devon.

The dawn rolled up as they went on their way towards Breezeton—and the factory chimneys were belching but smoke in the towns.

Sitting very quietly in her comer of the railway carriage, Jill Was realising much in that dawn. She winced at some things she realised. The biggest irony was to know that she was beginning to lose her interest in Firstlings. It had been half an impulse, half a fad, and she was not made of the stuff that can go on working and building when the impulse is gone, just as though it were there.

As soon as the personal element had come again into her life the Guest House had been less to her, the mothers had been less to her.

But Jill meant to keep Firstlings on, at all costs, as she sat in her corner, squaring accounts with herself. She was going to pile herself up with work, *that* work, though it did not seem to matter to her any more, in her sad little soul. She was going to make Firstlings a happy place, though she was not contented. And her chief reason for doing this was because William Mason had built it, and the other reason was—Jill was growing into a woman, who saw that she must carry out what her childish hands had set themselves to do—because the building of Firstlings, the opening of Firstlings by the "mother of eight," was a thing she could not go back on.

To go back on anyone like Mrs. Briggs, Jill knew, would be nothing short of treachery. And then—all the others, too! Even Martha Smith, even the mother of nineteen. As she thought of her Jill realised that she had quite forgotten to call on the mother of nineteen! It was an omission she made a note of. For Jill meant to be very hard on herself.

CHAPTER XII

MR. WICKS COMES ON BUSINESS

Jill and Mrs. Williams reached Breezeton just as the brickworkers were entraining for their day's work. The flowers and leaves blown about the country platform cast a sad sweetness on the air. Jill felt that she would have known that Mandy was dead, even had she arrived at this place without getting the telegram.

When she took the turn of the lane that she had come up with Giles and Mason just seven months ago her heart was very full. They could see the farm-gate over which Mandy would never lean again. All the white blinds were down. Two crimson hollyhocks swayed and burned in the sunshine. Mandy had been very proud of them. They were alive. But Mandy was dead.

Giles came out when he heard the gate creak. His arm was in a sling, and—he looked more than a week older since Jill saw him. But he was very cheerful, and spoke about Mandy as though she were still alive, seeming to get comfort from the very fact of talking about her to someone who loved her.

It was only when Jill saw him smoking the pipe Mandy had bought him for twopence in town—a colouring pipe which piles proudly said was often taken for meerschaum—that Jill realised that Giles was a little of a hypocrite too. He was smoking it with the bowl upside down—and never a whiff of smoke to come out.

Jill sent Mrs. Williams on to Firstlings alone. She stayed with Giles. That evening they came to measure Mandy for her shroud. Jill stood by whilst they did it. Some of the quiet calm from Mandy's face stole into her soul. Perhaps, always, when, she thought of Mandy in the old-fashioned house, so quiet and calm, and full of quaint ways she would experience that consciousness of being near Mandy.

Wherever Jill turned Mandy's personality had stamped itself. The buffet, upholstered with an old coat of Giles's—the parcel of clothes packed up and addressed ready to send to the mother of nineteen—the kitten inside the fender, being "brought up" to send to the Vicarage—the apples spread out on the store- room floor, just as Mandy had laid them, on clean newspapers. Jill got a curious comfort front going about, Seeing this touch from the hand that had done its last bit of woman's work.

After tea that evening she filled "Uncle" Giles's pipe, as she had seen Mandy do.

Giles told her how Mandy had sat down in the chair and just fallen asleep. He had known for some time that she had a "murmur," a heart weakness.

"Do you think that the extra work at Firstlings —?" hazarded Jill.

Giles shook his head.

"That give her joy," he said firmly, "an' joy never killed nobody—not in this World. No. Her time had come. Her time had come."

They laid Mandy in the earth two days later. Giles had now no one to "tent" the old house for him. He made up his mind to sell it up, and go to live with his oldest son, in Nottingham, who was quite a successful business man.

Jill claimed as her purchases the old buffet Mandy had made, Mandy's spectacles and spectacle-case, and a green sock, half-knitted, with the needles in it.

Jill thought a little chokily that if her eyes looked through Mandy's spectacles, at the same age, and saw as kindly and good a world, life would not have treated her so badly.

Henceforth the buffet and the spectacle case were kept in Jill's little room.

They were to remind her, in her struggles, of the serene old presence she had used to invite in, to rest and counsel her.

Jiff felt years older now that presence was no longer there. Firstlings pressed more heavily on her shoulders. She felt her responsibility as she had never done before.

Rain set in midway in the week that the Giles farm was empty. Wind and rain brought the leaves down faster. One or two of the women began to mope, now that the weather was bad. Jill, sitting in the blue room, in her black frock, her tired feet on Mandy's buffet, wondered what Mandy would have advised. It came to her at once. Mandy would have lit a big fire in the common room, and have set them toasting apples on threads before the bars.

Jill gave Martha directions to light the fire. Then she went into the store-room and brought down a huge basket of apples—apples which she herself had helped Mandy to shake down.

When the women came in, they found Jill with the tables full of apples—and stared.

"We are just going to sit around the fire," said Jill, "and toast our toes—and apples. Who'll thread the stalks? And somebody draw the blinds."

Ten minutes later the room hummed to laughter and talk. Four apples suspended on threads dangled before the fire. Somebody would give them a twist now and again. From outside came the sound of wind and rain.

"Winter's set in," said somebody.

Which made someone else talk of Christmas, which led to Christmas tales, and—ghost tales. Then Janet Burns started in to tell a Scottish ghost tale, with her little interjection of "Do ye ken?" coming in comically at the most weird parts. Then Mrs. Williams told a tale of the Welsh mountains—with the flash in her eye that made her look a little wild, and made Jill love her.

Martha Smith had no ghosts. She told a tale of the hardest Christmas she had ever had—a miserable, sordid little story—with a swear-word or two illustrating it—and something else—some softening of her heart that thus poured itself out on a fireside throng.

"If I'd known! " said the Northumberland woman who had come in Jill's absence.

"Do ye ken, we could help ane anither a lot, if we knew," said Janet Burns.

Tale after tale went round.

Apple after apple was eaten, and another hung on a thread to splutter and smell delicious. Sometimes a thread got burnt through and bang went the apple on the hearth that reflected a fire in every tile.

The freemasonry of motherhood, of struggle, of understanding, made it into a magic circle. When Jill told Mandy's tale of Mandy as a child, climbing the hill to find gold and bringing down broom, only to find it would not buy anything, it was almost as if Mandy *were* in the room. They started to talk of all the wonderful things their children said. This was really against the rules, the unwritten rules of Firstlings. For one of the committee had said that the mothers should be encouraged to follow new lines rather than the old ones.

But Jill did not discourage the line the conversation was taking. Never had the mothers been so happy. There was a little jealousy, of course, But the eagerness in every woman's face to tell of her child's cleverness— the time when somebody laughed—the intense look of waiting, to get a word in edgeways—and over all was the glow of the fireshine, the sense of comfort and well-being, the spitting sound of the apples, the little table with its fourteen candlesticks, all with candles waiting whitely to lead into soft, clean beds of utter rest for tired mothers, all getting fitter to go back and battle joyfully in their world.

Only Mary Williams sat silent amidst all this babble of children's sayings and doings. Jill went and sat next her. She remembered the little dead babies, one after one, for so many years.

Martha Smith went out to get the glasses of milk.

As they sipped the milk Jill made up her mind afresh that there could be no such thing as shutting up Firstlings, not even in the winter months. Tired as she was, there was no chance of a rest. She had no right to rest.

It seemed to her that she would be shutting the door of joy on so many tired faces!

She went to bed.

She was up quite early in the morning, to see that breakfast was ready, and all in what Mandy had used to call "apple-pie" order. It was still raining. The garden was beaten by the storm and the hills all about were veiled in mist. The lowing of the cattle came up mournfully from the fields.

From the breakfast conversation Jill perceived that the mothers did not know what to do with themselves that day. She remembered a covered bus that passed through the village at noon and went on to town. She broached the subject. The idea caught fire.

At noon twelve mothers, with six umbrellas and two pairs of goloshes amongst them, went down the hill to get the bus outside the inn where Mason had slept on that night when Jill had written:—

"This is the House that Jill built:

"These are the dreams that lay in the house
    that Jill built."

Jill watched them from the window.

Their laughter always made her feel sad for them. When they forgot and forgave the wrongs poverty had done to their motherhood, Jill was always least disposed to forget and forgive those wrongs, which is not only human but Irish. There was one little woman trudging along in Jill's goloshes who had not had a holiday before for twenty years, and that had been only for a day.

Janet Burns remained behind—to have high tea ready for the others on their return from town. The Tyneside mother had also stayed behind. Her asthma was bad with the change in the weather. She was smoking stramonium cigarettes in her bedroom. Jill had succeeded in persuading her that there was no dissipation in smoking herbal cigarettes.

Jill had the old ache at the nape of her neck.

She went into the kitchen to help Janet.

"I ken ye're not feelin' sae weel," said Janet. "Sit doon, an' I'll gie ye a cup o' tea. I've a bairn mysel' that's barely done growin'."

And Jill perceived, to her great astonishment, that Janet was daring to mother the self-elected mother of the mothers. For a moment she resented it. Nobody fussed Jill only Mandy, and Mandy was dead.

Jill's heart and head had felt bursting these last days. The problem of Harry Thorn and Mason felt too much for her. She had need of some confessional. There was no one to confide in. There had only been Mandy she could confide in.

There was quite a pile of letters for Jill—and one parcel, comical in shape.

It contained a crochet-covered pincushion from Mrs. Briggs, a gift that warmed Jill's heart as did the letter. There was also actually a note from Mr. Briggs, saying he had got a new wife back for an old. There was a letter from Mrs. Hamer, of the nineteen, and a photograph taken by an amateur, in the back-yard, of all the children, like steps, each one a little higher than the other, and in their midst a smiling little mother. Mrs. Hamer was a perfect cure. She would never as long as she lived forget that night when she had walked to get a mile nearer to the children she had run away from.

Jill laid the letter and photograph down with a smile. Several more women wanted to come, when there were vacancies. Jill had expected a letter from Mr. Wicks. It did not come until just before the mothers arrived back.

Jill could not quite understand it.

It said that Mr. Wicks was coming—to see her.

But she had no time to wonder what he could be coming all this way about. The mothers trooped in loaded with purchases from the town market—things to "make up" for the children at home. Jill could tell that some of them, happy as they were, were burning to get home.

What a bustle was that before tea was served. Jill was glad now of that rule that every woman brought a pair of slippers. Their muddy boots and wet clothes were left in the "drying-room"—where a great rack was waiting against a ceiling warm from a huge fire. There was great fun at the tea-table and some secrecy—little nods and winks and sly gestures.

Jill understood what this meant when she was presented with a fine china rose-bowl.

Jill behaved exactly as she ought to have done, and everybody was delighted.

"You'll happen think of us when that's full o' roses, ah' you're pullin' on a cradle-string," said a Wigan woman, with a broad tender smile.

Jill did not show that she had winced.

More and more she was realising that they were rich compared with what she would be when she reached their years. They had their children. "Hoined" they might be. Worn they might be. But joy went with the sorrow, and fulfilment with their struggle. She felt more akin that evening to the little Welshwoman than anyone else there.

The little Welshwoman could only bear dead babies. Jill was seeing herself spending her life mothering the tired mothers of living babies, and—wearing Mandy's spectacles. Jill knew herself for an old maid. She felt its imprint upon her. As they sat with the many lamps lit in the drawing-room, all sewing away, after Jill had cut things out for them, Jill felt that she was already quite old and grey and submissive to the inevitable. She was making an infant's chemise of soft silk, to the admiration of the mothers—when the bell rang.

It was Martha Smith's turn to answer the bell.

She came shortly afterwards to the door and looked in where Jill sat, like a very Dorcas, surrounded by mothers, while Janet Bums, who had been an embroideress at one time, was showing new stitches to about half-a-dozen round her chair.

"It's a Mr. Wicks, Miss Bennett," said she.

CHAPTER XIII

JILL GROWS DESPERATE

Jill went down the hall, where the big fire was lit and the hearthstone bright.

In the big chair by the fire sat Mr. Wicks. He was steaming—actually steaming—without being conscious of it.

"You've brought grand weather!" said Jill.

She could hear the rain tippling down outside.

Mr. Wicks looked at her agitatedly. He arose, still steaming.

"I've bad news," he said.

Jill's brain had got obsessed with deaths. Had she not said she had buried Harry? Miss Wheeler was dead, and so was Mandy. Jill was getting nervous.

"It's not— Mr. Mason is quite well?" said Jill. Then she could have bitten her tongue out, for she had caught a look of pleased surprise in Mr. Wicks's eyes, coupled with a lightening of the brows.

"Oh, no, he's quite well," he said; "but got jilted or something by his cousin. Anyhow, I never saw him look better."

Jill received a shock at this point. But she saw Mr. Wicks had not come about that.

She was about to ask him to get his wet clothes off when she remembered that there were no male garments in the establishment.

So she even allowed him to sit down again—and steam. All the time Mr. Wicks talked there was a cloud of steam rising from him. There was a steam outline of him, and steam rising from his hat, which he twirled in his hands.

"You mean?"—began Jill, aghast.

Mr. Wicks brought out a wet pocket-book.

Out of that came a scrap of newspaper.

Jill knelt down to read it by the hall-fire.

But the words swam.

"My dear young lady," said Mr. "Wicks, "you've lost your money. These embezzlers *never* refund it. Hundreds of old people are ruined by this, their life's savings gone. And—I thought—it was so *safe*, so very *safe*. I am sorry."

"It was my fault," said Jill. "I wanted more interest so that I could take in more mothers: I suppose—this means—Firstlings must close."

From the drawing-room came the buzz of happy voices. Jill looked what she felt—sick, even whilst something in her realised that this would liberate her from her vow; set her free to go and eat her heart out; for she was now apparently engaged to Harry Thorn, whilst Mason had got free of Susan.

"There is one other alternative," said Mr. Wicks out of a great cloud of steam that almost hid him.

Jill looked questioningly at him.

"On condition that you married—a—a relative of your uncle's," said Mr. Wicks, "he left you all he had."

"A relative?" queried Jill.

Mr. Wicks nodded.

"Fifty thousand pounds," said Mr. Wicks, "is not to be sneezed at."

He sneezed himself at this point, which made Jill smile, and realise that he was taking cold.

Martha Smith slept in the kitchen that night. Mr. Wicks' clothes hung in the drying-room. Mr. Wicks was a little uneasy as to whether they would remember to bring him his clothes in the morning. But on the whole he had pleasant thoughts, for he had seen that Jill was very bent on keeping Firstlings, which meant there was a chance of her accepting Mason.

* * * * *

On the morrow Mr. Wicks went back. He could not be persuaded to stop, but Jill got him to go back with Martha Smith for "company," which he very regretfully did. Martha's husband was sick; at least she had received a telegram to that effect, though Jill had good grounds to suspect that Martha wanted to go back.

Jill had promised to see if something could not be done for little Beatrice in the way of going into a school for the blind. Martha tried to say something as the train steamed out with Jill waving her hand, but she could not. But Jill's face said that she quite understood. Martha was taking the parcel for the "mother of nineteen" with her own hands.

Mrs. Williams took her place in the, kitchen. The house seemed very quiet without Martha's loud voice and aggressiveness.

Jill walked back to Firstlings very thoughtfully. She was thinking of the thing Mr. Wicks had hinted at. She could not close Firstlings.

Jill's face was so determined that one of the mothers asked her if something was the matter when she got back. Jill smiled and shook her head, vanishing into her own little room.

A great struggle was going on in Jill's mind. She was considering the question of sacrifice—sacrifice which had always seemed idiotic to her in story-books, where a young girl married an old man to save her family. Round and round the whole question went Jill, but she could not make up her mind. At length she put her feet on Mandy's buffet, and Mandy's spectacles on her nose, to see if that would help.

It was for the sake of a big family.

It was for scores of mothers who were always sacrificing. Jill thought of the newspaper paragraph that would appear saying her scheme had been a failure, or of its being wire-pulled by charity-mongers, and of those letters waiting to be answered from a hundred mothers in dingy streets.

Curiously enough, it was Mason's face that seemed to look at her reproachfully. Jill was angry with Mason. He must have jilted his cousin, she thought.

On the third day, quite worn out, in the privacy of her own room, Jill tossed up a crooked sixpence Mandy had kept for luck.

She looked down with frightened eyes at the coin. It was not "heads." She was to marry that relation of Uncle Birch's, that old man who would wake up with rheum in the corners of his eyes, as she had seen it in Giles's in the early mornings. Jill shuddered inwardly at the vision. It never dawned on her that her old uncle had any young relations.

But at least the uncertainty was over. She had saved her family.

Harry Thorn received a letter from Jill telling him she broke off the "dummy" engagement. He walked about a little, but was not quite so broken-hearted as he had thought he should be.

He wrote at once to Susan James and acquainted her of the fact. He had spent a few days showing Susan

London, for Susan had not gone back just when Jill did, after all.

Jill waited tensely for the answer to-the letter she sent Mr. Wicks by the same post that she sent Harry his *conge*.

It was ten days before it came.

There had been a great reshuffle of mothers. Jill was starting to get to know new ones—all but Mrs. Williams, whom Jill begged to stay on, and her husband, pleased by her photograph, begged her to stay on also.

Mrs. Williams was doing her "exercises," to get fit, when Jill tapped one night, and said, "May I come in?"

Mrs. Williams opened the door. Jill entered the bedroom.

"I—I am going to be married," said Jill, sitting on the bed.

"Oh—Firstlings will perhaps—" began Mrs. Williams.

"Firstlings will go on for ever," said Jill, stoutly.

They spoke very low. The candlelight shone on Jill, with her sacrificial look.

There was a silence.

"Do—do *all* old men have rheum in their eyes of a morning?" asked Jill, anxiously. Then she explained.

"You are going to marry an old man!" gasped Mrs. Williams. Then: "What about Mr. Thorn?"

"I have given him up," said Jill, without anything in her tone to say that she felt the loss.

"Oh, my poor dear!" said Mrs. Williams.

"It was a mistake," said Jill. "Anyhow, that's not important.But—do they—old men?"

She looked distressfully at her friend. Gradually Mrs. Williams got some parts of the tale—those which Jill chose to tell her.

"Then—he may not be old," said she.

Jill stared.

"Oh, I couldn't tolerate him for a minute if he wasn't!" she said, illogically.

It was on the next day that Mr. Wicks' letter came:—

"Have arranged for an interview between Mr. Birch's relative and yourself. Will meet the 2.30 train on Saturday."

When she set out on that eventful journey she told herself that she was not excited. She did feel quite unusually calm. But a sleepless night had made the old pain at the nape of the neck more acute.

"Oh here you are!" said Mr. Wicks, cheerfully, as he found her.

"Is he under seventy?" she asked once, as they sat back in the taxi.

"A little," said Mr. Wicks. His eyes winked in their odd manner as they did when he was amused.

"What will happen to the—the money—if I don't take him?" asked Jill.

"In that case," remarked Mr. Wicks, "*he is to have it all.*"

"I see," said Jill, in a way that said she did not see at all. Then she said, "You will think I'm a money-grabber, Mr. Wicks."

Mr. Wicks had much ado to keep his countenance grave as the young woman of the sacrificial look and the eyes that said she had lost some sleep put this query.

"Mrs. Wicks wishes you both to go to tea," he said, as they stepped out near his office. "Mrs. Wicks is very fond of you, my dear."

"Does she know him?" asked Jill.

Then she said, without waiting for an answer, "If I take him—do I get half?"

She looked at him anxiously. He could see she was mentally weighing that bag with twenty-five thousand pounds in it in her small hand, against—her repulsion against that old man, just under seventy.

Mr. Wicks could hardly contain himself. He was quite giddy in his manner of going up those steps Jill remembered so well.

He made Jill a cup of tea on his own spirit-lamp. A clock outside struck three. Jill started nervously at the sound.

Then steps came slowly up the stairs. Jill scarcely noticed them. She was feeling that she wanted to run away.

Someone tapped at the door, opened it, and in came Mason!

CHAPTER XIV

FIRSTLINGS IN PAWN

Will Mason started back when he saw Jill. Jill nodded rather distantly. Even then it did not enter her head that this was the "relative" she was to marry.

Mr. Wicks was opening the safe. He spread out some papers on the table.

"My dear young people," said Mr. Wicks, "I will proceed to read to you the will of your mutual benefactor—"

Then he saw Jill's eyes. They startled him. She was looking at Mason.

"Do you mean—" she said, almost hysterically.

Mr. Wicks tapped her hand. Mason was studying the floor-pattern.

"She expected to have to marry some old, old man," smiled Mr. Wicks, "whilst I have reason to believe this will be a pleasant sur—"

He did not get any further. Jill had leapt to her feet. Her look electrified Mr. Wicks.

At first she could get nothing out articulate. Then she spoke to some purpose.

"Not for twenty-five millions," she said. "Not to save ten thousand mothers. Oh! To think anyone could think that of me! He can have it. He can have it all!"

"Your answer is—"

"No!" said Jill shakily. "No, no, no!" When Mr. Wicks realised the situation Jill was at the foot of the stairs.

"Dear me!" said Mr. Wicks.

Mason was still studying the floor-pattern. "Did you guess?" asked Mr. Wicks. Mason lifted his gaze.

"I—came to say 'No,' " he said, "until I saw—the lady. For my part—I am now quite agreeable."

"But—"

"She is going to marry me," said Mason. "Excuse me. I am rather in a hurry."

He ran down the steps. Jill had vanished. Hailing a taxi, he went direct to Euston. She was sitting on one of the hard-railed seats, gazing before her, in a demoralised attitude. She did not see him until he sat beside her.

"Why won't you marry me?" Jill heard.

"Because I won't," was the feminine reply.

"You came up to agree to marry an *old* man you had never seen," said Mason, "and yet—you won't have me?"

Their eyes met. Mason's had that look at which the lion had roared. Jill withstood it finely. Her Irish blood was roused.

"You could talk from now to Doomsday," she told Mason. "No matter what you said it would not move me."

There was no mistaking it.

A porter was going by, wheeling a pyramid of boxes.

"That's the stuff to give 'em!" he said, waggishly. He winked as he caught Jill's scornful look.

Mason went on talking very quietly, ignoring the porter's cheek. Jill knew that Harry would not have talked it out in such a place. She knew that Mason was splendid. That was why she would not have him. Between those two could come no suspicion of bargaining. Moreover, she knew that she would die before confessing to him that she had been jilted, and that she had not buried Harry.

"You came up to marry an old man, Jill," Mason told her. "And you won't have me."

There was silence.

"I know that the way must be clear," said Mason, alluding to Thorn. "Why won't you marry me? I know you like me."

As the cheeky porter would have said, that put the lid on!

Jill got up from her seat. She walked with dignity towards her platform. Mason, with a wry smile, picked up her valise, which she had forgotten. Jill found that he was an eloquent young man. Moreover, he told her that Susan had given him up; that Susan had known all the time—at least, been very sure—that the proposal was not for her, and after keeping him on the rack for a week had found him deadly dull and not worth keeping.

Jill answered not one word. Mason's assured way of saying that he knew she liked him had made her hate him. She was going to show him differently.

"Thanks," she said, when he got her a cup of tea before the train moved out.

"You have quite decided to turn me down, then?" he queried, looking up at her. "I have used all the eloquence I have. If I'd any more I'd use that."

"I—don't want you," said Jill.

Their two faces had the same look.

"Very well," said Mason.

He turned on his heel, lifted his cap—and Jill sat drinking tea out of the thick cup, suddenly remembering she had eaten no food since she left Firstlings.

She arrived at Breezeton on the edge of dark, and crept into her own room.

When she came out, an hour later, the first mother she saw was Mrs. Williams.

She ate supper, feeling that it would choke her. Then she tapped at Mrs. Williams's door. It opened, revealing the slight figure in the gymnastic suit and the hair shook loose round the small face.

Jill almost tumbled on the bed. She burst into tears, not unlike those in which she had mourned Mandy.

Mrs. Williams did not speak.

Then Jill said impetuously, "Say something."

"Was he—impossible?" asked Mrs. Williams. She stood like a sympathetic small child.

Jill laughed shakily."Quite," she answered.

She went out from the room without confiding in Mrs. Williams. Quite suddenly she found that she could not. Mrs. Williams would have known that Firstlings was tottering.

Two days later Mr. Wicks wrote to say that the time-limit for the acceptance of the terms of the will was Christmas.

Jill drew a deep breath, and set to work. First of all, she had the word "Private" put on the door of the little room. Jill did some thinking during the following week. After which she got a directory, and found out where all the "big pots" of the neighbourhood lived.

Jill, who had felt that she had no organising abilities, started to save Firstlings by believing she had some.

She wrote letters, letters galore, to the "big pots," telling them of the great work that was being done at Firstlings.

She made appointments. She trudged up and down the roads to big houses—and got a few promises of help. In the meantime there was just a five weeks' run before her stock of money was gone. The mothers ate and were happy, not realising how the foundations of Firstlings were shaking.

Jill was indeed getting the tired look of a mother "fending" for her children.

At the end of a month the first contribution came in. It was a five pound note. Jill's stipulation that all money should be given unconditionally had been a great drawback. People wanted to see their names in print as givers, and to be on the committee.

Another week—and Jill sent out undignified letters, asking for aid. It was now a case of making ends meet indeed. And with a desperate courage born of her necessity Jill began to get stuff "on credit." She did it quite easily. Indeed, it was easier than she would have supposed possible.

Snow began to come down. The hills were white. Firstlings had a white roof. Snow picnics were organised.

Never had there been such a jolly time since the opening. Every day the mothers were out in the array of goloshes Jill had got from town. In the evenings they sewed or had informal concerts, at which Jill assisted, giving no clue to her secret knowledge that any crisis was approaching. Jill was less like a child these days than ever she was before or after. Bills of surprising amounts were filed neatly in the little blue room.

Sometimes she stared at the picture of "A Rainy Day" over the fire-shelf for quite a long time without seeing anything on it.

But it was when a small round-faced boy arrived, saying, "I've called for Benson's," that Jill realised she had not the courage to dive into debt, not even for Firstlings. She was only a wader. She told him so coolly though, that she would be in town next week, that he did not suspect that Jill had not twenty-five pounds.

Fourteen mothers, all cheerfully "eating their heads off," as Mandy would have put it, needed some keeping up with when interest had stopped dead. There were times when Jill felt she could have strangled the man who had absconded with her money; though to do her justice, she was thinking less personally of the matter than anyone else would have done. She considered that he had robbed the mothers and those old people whose lifetimes' savings had been in the Council. But they had not caught him.

Meanwhile, every day the problem went worse. A wall was closing around Jill. As it closed she began to realise hysterically how young she was. Once she had a mad impulse to write to Mason for advice. But pride, and a fear that he might take it for another sort of submission withheld her.

At another time she thought of calling a committee meeting. But the idea of seeing the respective faces of the members when she told them that Firstlings was tottering—Firstlings, that was to "go on for ever"—frightened her.

Janet Burns began to say that Jill was anaemic, she thought, and advised that someone should help her with the secretarial duties. Whereupon Jill grew indignant, because she did not dare have anyone to share her "duties." More and more she grew desperately determined that this happy houseful of mothers should not know how things were, nor be made uncomfortable.

If the house had been old she might have shut it up for some mythical "repairs" while she thought out a solution. For Jill's trouble was that she could not think clearly. It seemed that there was a surge of life round about her little room that kept her from thinking. Someone was always knocking at the door. "Private" might have been a word without meaning.

"It is my own fault. I have no dignity," thought Jill, funnily. Neither had she, any more than a daisy.

The little ache was always at Jill's nape of the neck now. She woke every morning with a perception of a load on her heart, and, sitting up, dull-eyed, to put on her stockings, would realise it for *the debt*.

It was a humorous tale told by one of the mothers, of their having once pawned a gas- boiler belonging to their landlord, when her "old man" was sick, that gave Jill a clue and a ray of hope.

She went that very day to—pawn Firstlings!

CHAPTER XV

JILL GOES TO LONDON

Jill walked without noticing the way, or the hedges which mimicked the blossoms of May, or the red berries that flashed scarlet against a clear sapphire sky, or the way a friendly robin went hopping along behind the hedge to keep her company. Jill did not even notice the hills rising like white billows all around, against the sky.

In the town the snow was now mud, trodden by town feet. Jill found herself outside a little door where, in shabby lettering, she read the name of a solicitor, with an invitation to walk in. Jill obeyed it.

She went up steps that reminded her of the shabby stairs of Mrs. Greenwall. Whilst she realised that she was doing a mad thing in turning to a strange solicitor rather than to Mr. Wicks. But since her visit to London she had, in her mind, linked up Mr. Wicks with Mason in an intrigue to beat her pride, that paradoxical pride which was so odd in Jill's nature.

"Come in!" said a voice.

Jill went in. She sat down and told the solicitor her business.

He was a shrewd little man.

There was a big safe in the room, which made Jill wonder how it had been got inside that box-like space. The little man listened attentively.

"You want to mortgage your house," he asked.

Jill nodded.

He put a great many questions, and promised to come and see Firstlings soon. He went next day. Jill returned with him to town. And then she handed over the deeds of Firstlings, and saw them put inside the big safe, to a great turning of the knob, and went out, with five hundred pounds, and the feeling that she had pawned Firstlings, and that the very birds of the air knew it! It was a relief, anyhow.

When she got back she was exhausted with the relaxing of the string of suspense. She found old Giles by the hall fire, with a present of Christmas store—great onions for sage stuffings, and apples for the store-room, and boxes of what he called "Salt Annies," and a promise of oranges. Giles had come to see his old friends. He did not want to stay at Firstlings. They talked about Mandy, as Giles loved to talk of her, and of Christmas, and of Giles's grandchildren. Giles would not dine in the dining-room. But he had a pot of tea and sandwiches by the hall fire, talking to Jill.

It was at the tail-end of his visit that Giles let out the information that "that young fellow 'at built this place" was going out building to foreign parts early in the New Year.

Jill was on the alert instantly. She suspected that old Giles was being engineered to help to strike at that pride of hers.

But the innocence of Giles did away with that suspicion.

Jill heard him clamp out of the hall. She experienced mixed feelings. She heard the door close behind him. It was a dull sound.

She felt suddenly very tired—and a little faint, and the shadows in the hall assumed strange shapes, dancing about her great chair, where she was so tiny a figure.

"I am going to faint," thought Jill, suddenly. She leaped out of the chair. She fixed her mind on the counting of the different colours in the tilings.

Everything was in motion. So she sat down again, very cautiously. She tried deep breathing—then realised, with some amazement, that the recipe was for sea-sickness, not lovesickness. Jill said the word over mentally, with scorn.

The letter-box clicked. Jill went wearily. The faintness was passing away.

She brought the letter to read by the hall fire. It was from Mr. Wicks. She opened it, with the tightness back at her brain again.

She read it with difficulty. But at length its meaning became plain.

There was another clause in Uncle Birch's will. Unless, within a few weeks she agreed to marry Mason, not only did she lose twenty-five thousand, but he lost his share also—and the whole went to anti-vivisection, and the providing of lethal chambers for cats and dogs!

Jill sprang up out of the chair again. *Lethal chambers for cats and dogs!* When women—mothers—were being done out of their right to live!

She walked about quite a good deal until the feeling of faintness had passed, then, opening a little drawer, took out a tiny bottle of ammoniated quinine tablets and swallowed six, one after the other, as a piek-me-up!

"I shall have to look after myself," Jill told herself firmly.

Never was any girl less fitted to look after herself than Jill, Jill who wanted to stretch protecting wings over all the sick and sorry lives in the universe.

Charles Lamb asserted that charity does not begin at home.

Jill did not assert it.

She proved it.

Jill had not thought of Mason being made poor by her quixotic refusal to marry him. Jill, as Thorn had sometimes said, did not "think." She went through the preliminary stage of thinking, and hopped over the intermediary step between that and action. It was her Irish blood that made her do that. The fact that she would lose Will Mason twenty-five thousand pounds upset her very much, though the fact that she would lose the same only concerned her insomuch as it affected the destinies of Tired Mothers. On the top of that was the other unexpected blow she had received in the news that Mason was leaving England. Jill was a bundle of disturbed and contradictory emotions during the week following the ill news that Giles had brought. Then one of the mothers noticed that she was looking ill. That did it. Jill pulled herself together by recalling the family tradition that no Bennetts let themselves go to pieces over private griefs, that one of her ancestors had given his attention to the public weal whilst his own fortunes had been devastated.

Every night she dragged on until the last mother took her candlestick and said "goodnight," then Jill also took her candle, after seeing that the hall door was fastened securely. She never fastened the door now, threading her way in the dimness of the hall, without recalling the moment in which she and Will Mason had dedicated the house to the mothers, pouring libation upon the hearthstone.

All the ill-luck had come upon Firstlings through her careless dropping of the cup, Jill thought superstitiously.

Always, too, as she passed along the hall, that memory of Mason and herself, dedicating the house, made her say to herself miserably, "Yes. *It* began then." For Jill no longer denied to herself the fact that she cared for Mason, cared for him more than she had ever cared for any human being, except her father.

She did not sleep much. When she did fall into an uneasy slumber, her dreams were of a grotesque character that made her smile on awakening. In one of her dreams she saw Mason putting out to sea on a raft, whereon stood his box, in which he had shut up the "mother of eight," who was trying to send a telegraphic message to Jill by beating a tattoo on the inside of the box with the stick which usually stirred the breakfast porridge at Firstlings.

Jill woke on this particular morning to find that someone was really knocking on her bedroom door.

"Coming," she assured the one who was knocking.

She had a very bad headache, and the feeling of depression that she always woke up with now. She had ceased to wonder, on awakening, why it felt as though someone were sitting on her chest. She knew the reason thereof, now, at once. Mason was leaving England.

Jill dragged herself out of bed and dressed, looking out of the window, as was her way. Morning mist rolled to the foot of Firstlings Hill. Through it, the naked trees rose as though they grew out of a white flood, like spume of the sea. It was almost uncannily beautiful. The sun was on the snow that came up to the garden edge, on the breast of the gleaming hill. Someone had made a snow man. He was leaned against the outside of the garden hedge, staring up at Jill with a grimace she did not like.

"If only I could ask *his* advice," mused Jill. "If only he were my friend." She was thinking of Mason.

Before going in to breakfast Jill stole for a few minutes into her sanctuary, the little blue room that surrounded one with the soft, warm feeling of a summer sky. It was the room furthest away from kitchen and dining-rooms. Everything was very quiet, the drip of ice- water from the window-ledge outside somehow seeming to make the stillness more deep.

Mandy's spectacles were laid on a copy of Palgrave's Golden Treasury. Jill sat down, held the steel-rimmed glasses in her hand, fondling them. Then she put them on, trying to believe that she was Mandy, trying to put on Mandy's wisdom, so that she might see clearly the good way out of the difficulties regarding Firstlings. It was all in vain.

Jill's prop of wisdom had been taken away from her. There was no Mandy. At least—

Jill's eyes filled, and her chin trembled. She felt more like the hackneyed and morbid "No-one-cares-for-me" than ever she had felt in her life.

During this chaotic period she had lost the illusion that Mandy was near her—an illusion which was common to her in this little blue room, associated with the memories of the pleasant old woman who had been the only person to sit there with her.

She could only remember that Will Mason had planned this den for her, its size, shape, and the exquisite colour, the one picture, even the round fat cushion to rest her feet, and the tiny chair. He had come between her and Mandy. She hated him most of all for that.

She left the little room, closing the door softly, as though leaving a church, and went towards the murmur of voices in the breakfast room, without her usual happy feeling of greeting.

Jill's family of mothers was beginning to be a terrible responsibility.

"Good morning," said Jill, wearily, on entering the breakfast room.

Her greeting included everybody.

She nodded to Mrs. Williams not to vacate her office as high chief server.

"Porridge?" queried Janet Burns of Jill.

Jill felt sick at the bare mention of porridge.

"Bacon?" asked Janet, briskly.

Jill shook her head.

"Marmalade?"

Janet looked a despairing "Don't say, no" at Jill.

"Just a little, Janet," answered Jill, whilst she wondered irritably, "What has it to do with her?" Jill, the most splendid owner of sheltering wings, grew restive when someone stretched a pair for her, just as she found it difficult to accept gifts, though she gave many.

Jill had sat down next to the Burnley woman, one of the latest arrivals at Firstlings, a huge person with pugilistic expression, who always spoke of her husband as "our Tom" and wore his photograph round her neck, in a huge gilded frame, dangling on the flowered pattern of her blouse, and reminding Jill of an enlargement on a parlour wall paper.

"I should give you black beer, if you were a lass o' mine," said Mrs. Robinson, supping her porridge noisily. This was after Jill had said grace, Mandy's grace, and the meal was in full swing.

Jill tried not to mind the loud noise of the porridge.

"I am a mean pig," she told herself miserably.

The mothers did not seem wonderful creatures to Jill, this morning. Everything was out of gear. Perplexed as to the future of Firstlings, selfishly disturbed because Will Mason was going away, she felt overburdened by her family. Firstlings was tottering. Yet they talked, laughed, read letters from home, with such absolutely selfish joy that Jill wanted to smack them, even whilst she knew that she could not expect them to be sympathetic about a trouble they did not know she was enduring.

It was the idea of what would happen if she smacked the Burnley woman that brought Jill's sense of humour into play.

A burst of sunshine filled the beautiful room with radiance, reflection from the pure white of the drifted snow outside. Jill looked across the table and out through the window. On a little knoll of utter brilliance woven of sunshine and snow, hopped a robin, looking for crumbs from Firstlings' tablecloth. In one flashing feeling it was borne on Jill that the mothers were hungry robins, too, picking up crumbs of joy and beauty, crumbs that should last them as long as their lives, crumbs to be sanctified into memories, happy memories, which all the sordid struggle of the ready-made existences they would go back to would never be able to mildew. She felt meaner than ever to have wavered in her love for them, and thought it must be the same feeling of being disloyal to her brood which had driven the mother of nineteen to try and walk back to them.

She was determined to get Firstlings out of pawn. The only thing was—How?

The ache in her heart and head grew keener during the next few days. Never had she needed Mandy so much,—Mandy with her country faith, country courage, and country wisdom.

It was after the worst night Jill had experienced (not excepting even that when Harry Thorn had jilted her) that she lay in bed, feeling no desire to go to face the mockery of breakfast, when she heard Mrs. Williams' gentle tap on the door.

"Come in," called Jill, without moving.

Mrs. Williams came in, and sat down on the little white chair by the little white bed that threw its reflection in the mirror of the white wardrobe at its foot.

"You look like you've been in a shipwreck," was the Welsh-woman's remark.

"I'm in one," admitted Jill.

Mrs. Williams waited. She had got to know Jill by this time. She guessed now why Jill had been able to sever her engagement with Thorn so easily.

"It's Mr. Mason worrying you," she hazarded when Jill did not proceed with the conversation.

Jill kept silence.

"You love him," began Mrs. Williams. "Why don't you—?"

Jill's look checked her further utterance. That young woman leaped up in bed, swift as a flash of lightning, giving the pillow a vigorous bang with her small fist. Her hair was tossed about her face, and her eyes were almost black in their intensity of feeling.

"Good gracious!" ejaculated Jill, in a disgusted tone. "Do you think that's what's the matter with me? Mr. Mason is a small affair."

She almost choked in her indignation, but Mrs. Williams did not look convinced.

"Well, then," said Jill, making up her mind, "it is not Mr. Mason, if you please. It's more than Mr. Mason.

He's young. He can fight his way—at least, he is not a mother. Mr. Mason indeed! I could push my personal feelings on one side—"

She checked herself, realising that she had admitted more than she meant to.

"I mean, if I *did* care for him," said Jill, with dignity, "I should not allow it to make me ill. I'll tell you what the trouble is—Firstlings is going down. At the longest it can only go on for two years—"

Mrs. Williams really thought that Jill was going to tear her hair, as she had once seen an Irishwoman do at a wake.

"Going down?" asked Mrs. Williams.

"Going down," answered Jill, with an irritability in her voice which Mrs. Williams had never heard there before.

She waved her hand at floor, roof and walls,—eloquently, looking not a little like that half-mad, half-genius of an Irish orator from which it was said the Bennetts had sprung.

"And it was to go on for ever and for ever," she said, in a despairing voice.

"I'm afraid I don't quite understand," murmured Mrs. Williams.

"We are sinking," Jill went on, "foundering—in a sea of debt. And I've found out that I can't bear debt. It killed Dad. He always said, 'Jill, never run into debt.' Never run into debt! Why, I've dived into it."

She got off the bed at this point and walked about the room, her nightdress trailing behind her like the robe of a tragedy queen.

"And I've tried all the big pots around," she added. "Oh, friend o' mine, how their superciliousness made my blood boil. They did not understand. They didn't understand the least little bit. They took Firstlings for a sort of Mrs. Barnardo's Home, and one of them asked me if I hadn't brought any envelopes to leave, as possibly they could do something."

Jill laughed at the recollection, but there were tears on her lashes.

"Do I look like- a philanthropist?"

Mrs. Williams almost jumped, so suddenly and fiercely did Jill put the question.

"Not just now," she said, dryly. "I should think you look more like a Fenian."

Mrs. Williams' idea of a Fenian was borrowed from her grandmother, who had once met someone who had seen a real one.

"Before they shall run it on conventional lines," said Jill, "Firstlings shall go down, the last brick of it eaten—we will go down fighting."

Which piece of Celtic metaphor tickled Mrs. Williams so much that she burst out laughing.

When she had recovered, she said merely, "How has Firstlings got into debt?"

"The man who had to do with the invested money absconded," said Jill, wearily. "If he had done it just to spite me he could not have put me in a worse hole. Yes. All the five thousand pounds was in it. It's no good crying about spilt milk. That was why—I went to London to see the 'old man.' It was Mr. Mason! Mr. Mason! Just think of it! He had come to marry any old frump, just for twenty-five thousand pounds,—of course, he was pleasantly surprised it was me. But, think of it, he had come to marry a woman who might be as old as his mother, if necessary."

"But you were prepared to marry an old man," said Mrs. Williams.

"He wasn't having to make a burnt offering of himself, was he?" sobbed Jill.

Mrs. Williams soothed her.

Jill told her everything, everything with the exception of the fact that Mason was going away, and taking her heart with him.

"We shall have to think of some scheme to get a few thousand," said Mrs. Williams, just as though it came naturally to speak of thousands.

"It ought to be easy," sniffed Jill. "It's such a b— big Ide—Idea. And there's money enough in the world. M—Mandy always said it was made round to go round. Why, only this morning I was reading of a young millionaire who has come to London and is just flinging money away like rain—"

She stared at Mrs. Williams in such a wild way, at this point, that Mrs. Williams thought she had got jaw-lock.

"I've got it," cried Jill.

She clapped her hands, and laughed like a gleeful child, even whilst her face was yet tear-blurred.

"Well, you are a weather-cock!" said Mrs. Williams, who was quite bewildered by this time.

"You don't mean to say," asked Jill, with provoking surprise, "that you've been wasting sympathy on me?"

"You—quite upset me," confessed Mrs. Williams.

"But I see a way out, "said Jill, tossing her hair back. "That millionaire! Why, we'll get him to rain a few thousands on Firstlings. I'll go to London and see him, at once. We mustn't let the grass grow under our feet. He had such a nice face in the newspaper. I'll tell him about the mothers—"

Jill was already walking on the heights.

Mrs. Williams tried to dissuade her. To the cool-headed Welshwoman it was a wild goose chase.

"You'll never get admittance to see him," she said.

Jill had already dragged her pilgrim's basket from under the bed.

Mrs. Williams gave up the idea of influencing Jill. There was evidently only one way for Jill to go, and that was her own.

But there was one jewel of memory Jill dropped, in compensation for all the helpless worry she had put on Mrs. Williams. It touched her inexpressibly. Jill never said, "Don't tell the others." She had taken Mrs. Williams into her confidence in the big way she did everything. Jill had not read the tales of the old Irish kings for nothing.

"If only she would marry that nice young man," thought Mrs. Williams miserably, after seeing the train off. "He would go her way, but she'd go along it in his way, without knowing it. Oh, dear! Well, perhaps she'll come across him in the street."

For Mrs. Williams had never lost her idea that London was only a kind of magnified village, where you could bang up against everybody you knew, if you only kept on walking.

Jill, sitting in the train, was trying to solve the question of where she would stay whilst in London. She would be most comfortable she knew, at Halgrove Chambers. But there was the danger that she might at any time meet Mason on the stairs, in her comings in and goings out. She did not want to meet Mason. She was quite sure of that.

She was going to see the millionaire.

It was 10 p.m. when the train got in at St. Pancras. After a few minutes of wavering, Jill decided to risk Halgrove Chambers, and hailing a taxi, got in, and was soon experiencing the delight of moving along through crowded streets, seeing the many lights, the odd shadows, the phantom shapes passing swiftly.

"I love people, crowds of them," murmured Jill to herself, as she let her head fall back against the cushions.

She got one of her brilliant ideas as her head was jogged mechanically by the motion of the vehicle.

"I'll bring all the mothers to London for a week, every single one of them," she decided, "if I get money out of that millionaire," Jill thought, in this Dick Turpin attitude of mind with which she had come to London.

The dream of bringing the mothers for a week's tour to London, even those who had already lived there (most of them knew only its poverty) to see its parks, picture galleries, Hampton Court, and to sail down the red sunset from Greenwich, past the pool with its picturesque craft, kept Jill happy.

"Halgrove Chambers," sang out the driver.

Jill stepped out.

That echoing silence which belonged to the Square fascinated her once more.

The man touched his cap as she walked away. His last fare had argued with him ten minutes. Jill had just over-balanced the opinion he had formed that women were niggardly and economical by nature.

Jill rang the bell and heard the Devonian caretaker descending the stairs. He came more slowly than usual, she fancied. Whilst she waited, she turned her back to the door and took note of the slim new moon, just gleaming through the naked trees whose leaves had been green when first Mason brought her to see Halgrove Chambers.

"It's only me," Jill announced herself to the Devonian. She had just finished turning her money for luck.

"Oh, Miss Jill," he exclaimed. "I'm afraid I was a long time, but I hurt my leg last week. Give me the basket, miss."

He shouldered it, despite Jill's protests, saying that carrying that bit o' thing could not possibly hurt his leg.

"Mr. Mason's away," he confided, on the top step.

"Oh, yes," said Jill, casually.

She was both surprised and annoyed that she did not experience quite so much relief as she ought to have felt at the coast being clear.

"Down in Devon," said the caretaker. "Gone to see his mother, before he leaves for foreign parts. It's sad about him, miss. My own opinion is that Miss James has fairly broken his heart by throwing him over the way she did, for Mr. Thorn. The change in him, miss! Why, he almost bit my head off once or twice when I joked him about his looks. Fair heart-rendering it were to see him."

"I hope your heart is better, Thomas," said Jill.

Thomas's corruption of "heart-rending" brought to Jill's mind that he had been suffering from fatty-heart, according to Mr. Wicks.

"Better, miss, thanks," said Thomas, appreciatively.

He set her basket down on the little green mat where she had once dropped the photograph of Harry. The deep-sunken door looked quite black in the shadows, for there was only the uncertain light of the hall lamp.

Jill unlocked the door and switched on the lights. The beauty of the picture-covered walls loomed out of the darkness to give sudden joy to Jill's heart.

She drew a deep breath, tossed off her hat, and Thomas withdrew. Before taking off her coat Jill lit the fire. She experienced a curious sense of lightness, as though she had laid a burden down. No one could burst in on her here. The clock on the fireshelf had stopped ticking, and she did not set it going. She wanted utter stillness.

It was as she ate supper that her wandering gaze caught sight of a letter which had half- slid under the carpet. She opened it, recognising Susan James' handwriting.

"Dear Jill" (ran the letter):

"Harry and I were married yesterday by special licence, and I am sure you will congratulate us. Owing to the many demands that will be made on my time I send in my resignation to the Committee, feeling certain that you will easily get a substitute. Give the mothers my love. By the way, what are you going to do about my cousin? I think you are treating him abominably, Jill. I saw him lately and he was quite changed, and it's all your fault. He told me something of the cause of it all, and I was surprised! Didn't think *you'd* let a little item like an old man making a bargain for you stop you marrying him. It is absurd. I could write you reams about my cousin Will, and then you would not know what you are throwing away. You would have to see him with his mother to know him really. He has the gentlest, noblest, bravest heart. (I write this with my blotting pad half-over, because Harry is a little jealous of Will. Perhaps he has need to be).

Jill, do not be a fool,—if you can help it. Do you know—his mother knows all about it? She cannot understand any woman not being willing to marry her boy. Of course she can't. She asked him if he could let her come from Devon to

London, or on to the North, to see you, and never in her life has she travelled anywhere, for she is a home-keeping woman. But Will said if he could not talk you round, his mother should not go courting for him.

(Jill gulped and laughed at the picture).

"Do marry him, Jill. Well, I must close. Think it over. If Will gets off, he will never come back. Well, Harry is calling to me. We are off to the office to bookkeep together. So, good-bye, dear Jill, and don't be silly. "Ever yours,

"Susan Thorn.

"P.S.—Anytime you like to come to tea, we shall be happy to see you."

Jill sat pondering this letter. She read parts of it over and over again. There was something between the lines that showed Susan in a better light than ever Jill had seen her—as an appreciator of some human being other than herself.

"I wonder if she was in love with him," thought Jill.

She read again the phrase that haunted her.

"He has the gentlest, noblest, bravest heart."

"And he would think I'd married him for the beastly money," said Jill. "And then I should have to tell him that I was once jilted."

It was the last fact which raised the insurmountable barrier. Jill could never think of the indignity she had suffered at the hands of Thorn without feeling that someone was pouring cold water down her back, and that she went quite white. It affected her as Irish music always affected her, save that the music softened her heart, whilst the recollection of Thorn's meanness built a wall around it.

She was just about to switch off the lights and go to bed when a tap came to her door.

"Excuse me, miss," said Thomas, "but I've had a wire. My brother is seriously ill. I shall have to go home. Do you mind being in the block alone just for a night? I've wired for the man who takes my place when I'm on holidays."

"I'm not the least bit afraid—" said Jill, smiling. "Where are the keys?"

Thomas handed them to her.

"And for extra safety, miss," he said, advancing into the room, "here's a revolver. It's all right, miss, it won't shoot, or I shouldn't have given it to you," he added smiling, "for you look as safe with it behind you as before you. But if you looked very grim, and angry, it might be effective."

"Thanks, Thomas," said Jill, meekly.

"Because—between you and me," said Thomas, lowering his voice, "Mr. Will has a picture worth two thousand pounds in his room. He had to buy it for a friend, and you never know. But a good clout on the head with that, and any burglar would lie still until you'd got the police."

"Oh, I'll be all right, Thomas," said Jill, hurriedly. Thomas was so matter of fact about the burglar chancing to call that Jill began to feel nervous.

"Eleven in the morning and the other man will be round," said Thomas. "Good night, miss."

"Good night," answered Jill.

She heard him stump his way down the steps, the clang of the door, then silence seemed to rash up the stairs. Jill did not go to bed soon, as she had intended. She sat, occasionally thinking of burglars, of being alone in the block. She wished Thomas had not told her of that valuable picture in Mason's room.

A cinder falling on the hearth made her jump.

Then she took herself in hand.

"Go to bed, Jill Bennett, it will soon be morning," she said, severely, to herself. She went. But she was nervous and could not resist a glance under the bed. To make herself feel more secure she put a box behind the door.

"There!" she said, triumphantly, "if any burglar tried to get in here, he'd have to knock part of the wall down to do it."

Jill-like, she had not thought that a burglar might happen to come through the window, her window, in all that block. She thought of Mandy, to make herself even more secure. To think of dear old Mandy was to have one's faith in human nature sweetened and made whole.

"How Mandy would have preached to a burglar!" thought Jill, with a laugh, under the bedclothes. "And then, she'd have given him a shilling, and an old suit of Giles's clothes and let him go, because he had a mother."

Quite suddenly, Jill began to sob, the sobs of a child with a full heart. The close memory of Mandy in all her pure and joyous goodness, had come close to her again, as it had not been for days. The tears cooled her tired, hot brain.

"I shall sleep to-night," Jill told herself, cuddling down into the pillow.

She had the electric switch close at hand, also the old revolver,—but the thing that made her feel most safe of all was the memory of Mandy, and Giles, and people like them, simple, kindly and true, all over the world.

CHAPTER XVI

JILL'S BURGLAR

About two o'clock Jill was disturbed by a noise, which was not loud enough to really awaken her. She turned over with a deep sigh, and did not open her eyes.

"Get up," commanded a voice, the tone of which annoyed her even in her semi-conscious state, so that she felt sleepy anger, and, rubbing her eyes, scrambled up in bed.

"I shall do nothing of the kind," Jill answered automatically, responding to that feeling of anger. The words ended in a slight scream. She had opened her eyes. Coming towards the bed was a dark figure whose shadowy outline gave an impression of youthful slimness.

He carried a lantern the light of which dazzled Jill.

He spoke.

"If you make any noise again, you'll be sorry, that's all."

It was a real live burglar.

"Now, get up, get something on, and make me a decent feed," he said.

Jill wanted to shout "Murder," though she had often thought no burglar would ever make her do such a thing. To her disgust she found herself obeying the man.

The burglar turned a little to one side whilst she slipped on her blue and apple blossom kimono, tremblingly fumbling after the wide sleeves.

"A gentleman, too," thought Jill.

Then she lashed herself for her fear.

"Coward, coward, coward!" she upbraided herself as she pulled the belt around her.

"Do you mind waiting until I put my slippers on?" she asked. The words lost some of their courageousness, through sounding as if they had been chewed by her chattering teeth.

If Jill had not been so nervous she might have noticed that the burglar started on hearing her voice for the second time and then he studied her countenance keenly.

"Certainly not. I should not like you to take cold," he said with polite satire.

Jill kept her gaze upon him whilst she fumbled after her slippers, much as one might watch a dog that might bite at any moment.

She was irritated that she could not get them on.

"What's that?" asked the burglar, brusquely, nodding towards the trunk behind the door.

"The box I put there to keep you out," Jill answered him. Her voice was not so choppy now.

"She will try to wire for the police," was his inward comment. "Who would have thought little Jill would grow into *this?*"

"What is there in it?" he asked, with the coldly official air of a customs house officer.

"Crinoline, poke bonnet, Paisley shawl, belonging to my granny, who is dead," said Jill, solemnly.

"Open the box," he commanded, unbelievingly.

Jill lifted the lid, a scent of dead lavender, old muslin, greeting their nostrils.

"Anything else?" he asked.

"No cigarettes, whisky, or Eau de Cologne," avowed Jill.

"You will find this is anything but a joke before you have done." said the polite burglar.

He put the lid down gently, and with one hand lifted it by the handle from the doorway, never taking his glance from the figure in the kimono dressing gown.

"No, you don't," he said quickly.

For Jill had guessed that the draught she felt was coming in through the mutilated window, and had been unable to resist the temptation of moving towards it, in hope to shout for help.

He opened the door for her, and drove her before him—like a sheep, thought Jill, in a rage. Moreover, she had forgotten the revolver Thomas had given her to clout any midnight visitor with.

"At least we can have a light on the subject," said Jill, midway on the stairs, and pressed a button which the burglar had not suspected was there. She turned and faced him, and received a shock.

"Geoffrey Barnes!" exclaimed Jill.

"Proceed into the dining-room," said Barnes, casually, but he had winced at being recognised.

"I wondered where you got to when you left the office—" murmured Jill, stepping forwards.

Barnes was eyeing the doors and windows, now that the room was lighted.

"I've done six months for burglary and assault," explained Geoffrey.

"What a shame!" said Jill, but it was not clear whether her sympathy was for the sufferers from the crime or the criminal.

Jill was no longer alarmed. Geoffrey Barnes had been kind to her when first she came up to London from Breezeton to work in a city office. He had been the one who corrected her shorthand notes, and once he had taken her to see "Where The Rainbow Ends" along with a woman whom Jill remembered as a cross between a fine lady and a fairy, scarcely of flesh and blood. The fairy lady had said the play was charming, but Jill had always thought that she was really bored.

"Be as quick as you can, Jill," said Barnes.

He sat down in the big chair that had been her old uncle's, after assuring himself that the heavy curtains let out no chink of light into the quiet square.

Jill spread out a snowy cloth on the mahogany table on which she had dined with Mason, when they had opened tinned apricots and she had talked whilst Mason poured the tea. Jill felt choky. Then her gaze fell on the picture of Mandy in her frilled cap and Sunday bodice, alongside another of a famous actress as Juliet. Mandy seemed all smiles.

In ten minutes, by the aid of the electric lamp, Jill had the kettle singing and the table set.

The burglar drew a chair up.

The sight of Mandy's picture had given Jill confidence. She could scarcely believe that Barnes would rob her—little Jill, whose notes he had corrected, whose tears he had once dried when she felt homesick for Breezeton and the dead father. But Jill was certainly anxious, though no longer alarmed. In her bag on the sideboard were fifty pounds in five pound Bank of England notes, along with her cheque book. Barnes had certainly changed very much since she had seen him last, though.

"If he takes my bag I shall fight him for it," thought Jill. It was her first really decisive idea. For to Jill that money did not belong to her so much as to the mothers. It was five weeks' house-keeping money for Firstlings, and she would fight for it, as women fight for their children's bread.

All this was in Jill's mind as she said quietly,

"What a long time it is since we went to 'Where The Rainbow Ends!'"

The gaze of her uninvited guest came back from surveyance of the plate behind the glass doors of the Indian cabinet, the top shelf of which was packed with curios.

"Oh that night at the theatre?" he said, as if he only remembered with an effort.

"Have you seen Miss Bland lately? "queried Jill.

Barnes' face grew dark, his expression bitter.

"Not lately—" he answered.

"I thought—" began Jill.

"Oh, she took the other fellow," said Barnes. "He had a motor car. She was always romantic."

"Have a bit of that cheese, and never mind," said Jill gently. "It's real Wensleydale."

There was certainly something tickling as well as touching in the way Jill handed Barnes the Wensleydale cheese in comfort for the loss of Miss Bland. Barnes eyed Jill, two sides of his nature battling together. The worse side came uppermost, because he was getting afraid of Jill.

"You seem to have done very well," he said. "Gone the easy way, eh?"

Jill blushed, then went very white.

"If I had been a man," said Jill, quietly, "you would not have dared to say that to me." She regarded him with a gleam of indignation.

I beg yours—I thought—" said Barnes.

"My uncle who is now dead, left me these rooms," Jill explained. "He also left me ten thousand pounds. Half of that has absconded—I mean a man has absconded with it. The other half I built a house with, for tired mothers. I've nothing in the world but these rooms and what they contain, and I've come up to beg for funds to carry on the Institution."

Barnes studied Jill as she spoke. He had thought she had become a pretty young woman, contrasting her with the girl who came in her black attire to work in the office. Now he substituted another word for "pretty"—a better word.

"Oh—so you could not set me on my feet," he said.

"I wish I could—yes, do have some more cheese," said Jill, leaning her head on her hand.

"Don't worry, I shall help myself," said Barnes, meaningly.

Jill's mouth set itself with determination. She tried not to look at her bag, the bag flung down so carelessly. Whilst all the time she was wondering if he could possibly know that behind a door on the other side of the passage was a picture worth two thousand pounds. She gave him his sixth cup of tea.

"That masterpiece of Rubens is somewhere in this block," said Barnes, suddenly. "Any idea of its whereabouts?"

Jill shook her head and stared.

"Little liar," said Barnes. He had seen her small hand clutch the table-cloth.

"You are going to find me that picture," said Barnes. "Now, no fooling. I'm a desperate man. I'm going to get out of England and live straight. This is the last time I'm on this game—and you are going to help me. So that should touch your tender little heart."

He laughed. Jill shook her head determinedly.

"I shall do no such thing," she said.

"So—you know where it is," he said, triumphantly.

"Yes, I do—in a way," said Jill, properly aroused.

She stuck to the table when Barnes tried to drag her away.

"Where is it?" he kept reiterating. "Tell me." Jill merely repeated, "I sha'n't."

Some rattle of a shutter not securely fastened gave him alarm. White and desperate he listened. Jill listened, too.

"It's nothing," she said. "Don't be frightened." He caught the sympathetic look on her face, and quite suddenly the humour and tragedy of the affair flashed on him. Jill, whom he was bullying and going to rob, was telling him no one was coming to catch him, just as though he were a pet rabbit. He grew afraid of himself, and his revulsion of feeling, before this creature so defiant yet pitying, so weak yet so strong.

There was no further sound. All was safe, as Jill had said. But he must be off—and he was not going without the picture that would give him a clean start.

He dragged her away from the table.

"You hurt my arms—" said Jill, childishly. "Please don't."

It made him feel an unutterable brute.

"Which room is it in?" queried Barnes.

"I sha'n't—" said Jill.

"You must go and show me—" he said.

She shook her head.

Sudden rage seized him. He flung her against the table. She stared at him in a dazed way and, quite forgetful of the tradition of the Bennetts, swayed and fell, catching her head on the corner of the table, shouting "Mandy, Mandy," just as she had used to shout when she tumbled, as a child, yet somehow knowing that Mandy was dead, and could not run to her.

When she opened her eyes, she was sitting in her uncle's chair. She rubbed her head and wondered why everything danced when she looked at it.

"I'm—I'm sorry, Jill," said Barnes.

He was standing some paces away looking at her.

"But where's the picture?" he asked.

"I shouldn't tell you if you killed me," said Jill, wearily.

"All right. I'll explore myself," said Barnes.

"Here!" called Jill, hurriedly, as he was leaving the room. "How much will it cost to get you out of the country?"

Barnes stared.

"There are men who would work their passage," suggested Jill, for she really did not feel that she had the right to start ex-burglars in life, at the expense of her mothers, or to cast their bread on the waters, even if it might return in many days.

Jill got up impulsively, stumbling once on her way to the Indian cabinet. She took down a bowl of beaten gold. She could help him without robbing the mothers.

"That's worth what would take you to the Antipodes," she told Barnes, "if you're afraid of stoking your way out. And this," she pulled a ring from her finger, "is worth fifty pounds. It's my only article of jewellery. You've youth, you've health, you've brains, and you aren't trammelled up in skirts and having to keep appearances up. Good Lord, man, if I were you, with the courage to break in folks' houses at dead o' night, and brains enough to dodge the law, I'd have made good inside five years, and shown that Bland woman I could run a motor car, and someone else in it, too. Look at some of those millionaires!" Jill's words came tumbling head over heels. Her eyes flashed and she was all animation, confidence, and scorn.

"It's a sign of weakness," Jill told Barnes, "to have to dodge a way to success by back doors, I mean windows, in the dark! If you want to get there, go straight—Anyhow, I'm sure I could. At least," she added, Irishly, "if anyone, successful, can be straight."

"Do you think I could?" he said.

"Sure," stated Jill.

"But—I've been in prison," he half groaned.

"The worst prisons we ever get into are those we build around ourselves," said Jill, looking like a Celtic priestess, for all the world. "If I'd been in prison twenty times, and decided I would not go there again, nobody'd make me. You've barred yourself in a prison of fear. Geoffrey Barnes, with your own hands, you've done that. Because you've done time for burglary you think you've to go on being a burglar. It's like saying you can't change your job."

Jill pushed the gold bowl towards him, held out the ring on the palm of her hand.

Geoffrey Barnes was looking at her with intent thoughtfulnesss.

"I'll do it, Jill," he said.

He had received an awful shock when he saw Jill fall, some minutes before.

"You're not starting straight off a crooked deal," said Jill, earnestly. "You're starting straight *this very minute,* and I do believe that a thing given with good wishes brings luck."

She laid the tiny ring or his hand. The man looked at it steadily, then smiled, and held it out to her, shaking his head.

"They are true stones, aren't they?" asked Jill.

"I'll not start off charity, anyhow," said Barnes.

"Charity!" said Jill, resentfully. "Why—I was never charitable in my life! That's fellowship! If you don't take it, you'll hang around London, trying to save enough to take you out, to get clean away—and you'll get tired. Get away. You can pay it back afterwards."

"You do talk like anybody's grandmother, Jill," said Barnes. His face was twitching a little. Then he started. There was the sound of a motor car outside, then the sound of a key turning in the lock, and steps were ascending the stairs. There was the sound of cheerful whistling. The cheerfulness of it annoyed Jill.

"I say—" began Barnes, white to the lips.

"You ceased to be a burglar five minutes ago," said Jill. But her own heart was beating fast. She knew it was Mason who was coming up the stairs.

"What am I, then?" asked Barnes.

"My friend," said Jill. "And that's a friend of mine who lives in rooms here."

"But—it's three in the morning," said Barnes. "Good gracious! Don't you realise?"—

"I realise," said Jill, in a low voice, "that I am just as respectable at three in the morning as at—" She faltered.

It was very hard to be thought ill of by Mason.

"Look here—I'll go back the way I came," said Barnes. Jill plucked him by the sleeve.

"Hello," came a voice outside the door.

"It's all right, Mr. Mason," said Jill. "I'm up rather late, having supper. Come in a moment, won't you? I've a friend—"

Mason had already seen the outline of a man.

He entered the room, saw the table, still set for two.

"Mr. Geoffrey Barnes—Mr. Mason," Jill said, sweetly. But she looked a little perturbed.

"I could drink a cup of tea," said Mason. "Been travelling all day."

Jill made him one.

Barnes began to look uneasy.

"I'll be off, Jill," he said at length.

Mason went downstairs to let him out. Jill heard the returning steps of the man whom she felt sure must have misjudged her. He had been a long time letting Barnes out.

Mason came in, smoking a cigarette, and stood on the hearth, back to the fire.

"I'm afraid you must think me—" began Jill. Mason was silent.

"—a little gay," added Jill, nervously.

Mason was still silent.

"As a matter of fact," said Jill, trying to speak calmly, "that was a burglar."

"He had soon learnt to call you Jill," mumbled Mason.

"I knew him before he changed into a burglar," explained Jill, incoherently. "But he didn't know it was me until he shone his light on me—anyhow, he is going out to Australia to start afresh. If you think he was anything else, see there—he did that."

She grabbed hold of Mason's hand impulsively, pushing her hair back at the temple with it. Her hair was clotted with blood, where she had struck the table.

"Here," said Mason, "that wants seeing to." It was funny and touching to Jill to see him pale at her hurt.

"Not at this time of the morning," said Jill, with dignity. "Good night."

He walked away, turning in the doorway. There was a smile on his face.

"I knew all the time," he said. "He told me at the door. He was afraid that you'd appear in a poor light. But if he hadn't said a word, Jill, if you hadn't, either,—I should have known it was all right."

Jill looked surprised.

"I'll come in to breakfast in the morning," said Mason, "and explain. It's three o'clock."

He waited on the little green mat until Jill fastened the door, with him outside.

Then he said, "I know you like me, Jill. Why won't you marry me?"

"It's three o'clock in the morning," said Jill, stiffly.

"Mrs. William Mason is a nice name," was his parting shot. "And you'll find me handy to deal with burglars."

Jill made up the fire.

She could not sleep, but rested in the big chair.

"Hello," cried Mason, briskly, at the dining-room door, about eight o'clock.

There was no answer.

"Hello!" he cried again.

He saw Jill's handkerchief, dropped in her early morning flight. He waited two hours, hoping that she had only overslept, and would come to make him some breakfast. But no Jill appeared. She had fled to the refuge of "lodgings," and he knew not where to seek her.

"They might well call the Irish the most provoking race on the face of the earth," pondered Mason. "I wish the old chap had left his money to cats and dogs outright." He went without breakfast, after all, and thought more pessimistic thoughts than ever he had done in his life. But he had one consolation. Jill's handkerchief, which he tucked inside his wallet, and dined off, at intervals.

As for Jill, not knowing exactly where to run, she ran to Mrs. Greenwall's, and Mrs. Greenwall was more than delighted to take her in. Soon afterwards, Mrs.

Greenwall had occasion to go out for food. Incidentally, she called at the local post office, and sent off a wire to Mr. William Mason. It ran:—

"Jill is here. Pleased to see you to tea.
GREENWALL."

Mason had been in touch with Jill's old landlady, and knew, "for sure, for certain," as Mrs. Greenwall put it, that Jill had been jilted—because she had come into money, and in good love-tales the young man always "gives you up when you come into money." Having met Harry, Mason was somewhat puzzled.

When he arrived at Mrs. Greenwall's, Jill had gone to the British Museum.

"I'll wait until she comes back," said Mason.

He had dinner with the Greenwalls, and waited a long time, enlivening his visit by reading "Pilgrim's Progress" in that room where Jill had once waited for Harry Thorn. He then had tea with the Greenwalls, when it was certain that Jill was not coming back to tea. Perhaps he looked more dejected than he knew.

"Have you ever read, "Worth The Waiting?" inquired Mrs. Greenwall, sympathetically.

Mason had not had the pleasure.

"It's a lovely tale," said Mrs. Greenwall, "and it might be my life story. You ought to read it. Mr. Greenwall had a long time to wait for me. And—look at us now."

Poor Mr. Greenwall did not look altogether happy.

Mason escaped at last from Mrs. Greenwall's confidences about the days of her youth, when, according to her own account, she had been just such another girl as Jill, though Mr. Greenwall's face showed no sign of recollecting it.

London was growing into a thing of mystic beauty—a thing of lights, shadows, sunset, and the blue running through the streets. Mason mused.

There were only ten days before his ship sailed. If he went, it would be, for him, .a ship that would never return. He had determined that. Jill had no human right to play with his happiness, just because of the barrier of twenty-five thousand pounds. If she did not give in before it was too late—she did not care sufficiently. That was plain. If she did not care sufficiently, he did not want her. Mason was proud, too.

It was clear that Jill was dodging him. He wondered what had brought her so hurriedly to London, and if she was staying long. He remembered what Mr. Wicks had told him of Jill's financial loss—and suspected her visit had something to do with that. He was more than sorry about Firstlings, for—he had built it, five hundred pounds of his was in its walls, unknown to Jill—and he had built the dream of his love into it, too. It seemed that like Firstlings, his dream must become a closed door. He walked on, unutterably lonely, seeing the throng about him only as shadows.

CHAPTER XVII

JILL CALLS ON A MILLIONAIRE

Jill had really intended to go to the British Museum. But as she was walking along the Tube sub-way, she saw a coloured poster advertising a honeymoon-topic revue. It reminded her of Susan and Harry Thorn. With one of the sudden changes of mood, all too common with her, of late, especially, she decided to take the lift into the street, get a bus, and call on the newly married couple. She had no difficulty in finding the tiny flat.

They received her with the cordiality that springs from real happiness. There was no mistaking the fact that Thorn thought a great deal of Susan, whilst Susan's way of saying "Toss me that cushion, Harry, please," or "Do you mind reaching me the teapot, dear?" convinced Jill that Susan had certainly the ability to manage a husband. For her own part, Jill knew she would despise any man who wanted managing. Jill was also amused by Susan's air of superior wisdom,—her "Sit by the fire, child," as though a wedding ring gave the wisdom of antiquity so soon as it was put on. But the one thing that showed how little real grip Harry Thorn had made on her own life was the absolute lack of jealousy the sight of their happiness caused her. The sudden idea seized her that if she had been called on to witness the happiness of Will Mason, in this fashion, she would have had to run out of the place.

She sat and admired everything, from the tea-tray to the silver-grey Persian kitten which Susan had actually named Jill, after her friend. Susan had thought of arousing a little pique in Jill, by exhibiting the new home, and had relished the idea. She felt a little ashamed of this as she handed tea to a soft-eyed Jill, so generous in her admiration, and, more like a tiny child than ever as she sat in the oak-panelled chair that really belonged to the Persian kitten.

It was very pleasant and quaint to Jill to see Susan pouring out tea from the new cups, in her new tea gown, and the new grey and green paper on the wall, decorated by Japanese pictures and Chinese pottery, and old-fashioned horticultural plates framed in ebony.

Susan had made the cakes, with Harry's help, she said, and Jill laughed, and Susan laughed, and Harry looked a little foolish, but was finally infected by their laughter and laughed, too.

"I should never have been able to make him laugh at himself," mused Jill. "Susan is wonderful."

"We are going to see 'Romeo and Juliet,'" said Susan, leaning across the little table, "do go with us."

Thorn looked quite relieved when Jill shook her head.

"An appointment," teased Susan, flashing a look at Jill's hat, which was certainly an expensive affair for Jill, being made of the leaves of French roses. It looked as if some fairy had dropped it on Jill's head.

Jill shook her head again. She could not tell Susan about having to beard the millionaire in his den, on behalf of the mothers. Jill felt that she could talk to no one but Mrs. Williams about the financial dilemma she was in.

"He sails in ten days," said Susan, irrelevantly, packing the things up on the tray, and tinkling a little cattle bell, for the Irish maid to come and carry them away.

Jill raised her eyebrows questioningly, and wondered why she had a speaking face since she did not intend to act for the films.

"Oh, you know whom I mean," said Susan, slyly. "I thought you had got that hat to captivate someone. Yes. It's true. He sails in ten days, unless—well, I'm awfully sorry for him, for it's leaking out all over the place that he's had a disappointment in love and is going away for his health. But I must congratulate you on the hat, dear. It's perfection." Susan's way of saying the last few words nettled Jill. She rose from the spindle-backed chair.

"In Natural History," she said with dignity, "the male birds put on the bright colours. I shall certainly never go forth to catch a man in a hat-trap."

At which Susan only laughed.

They went into the little dressing-room whilst Jill made her hair less unruly.

"You would be sorry for him if you could see him," said Susan. "The look on his face, Jill. Why—he looks as though he might jump into the Thames for two pins."

Jill peeped at herself in the glass.

"You need not fib so," she said. "I have seen him. He whistles most cheerfully and is quite brown."

She left the flat feeling that she was stepping out of a pretty nest of colour and light into a wide, lonely world. It was raining, too.

"I hate London," she mused, forgetting her recent rapture in the taxi, on her arrival in the city. "Nobody cares what you do. Really, it would make no difference what one did, except to one's self, and, after all, it's tiresome caring for one's self."

Jill was discovering that living for Tired Mothers was not all beer and skittles, particularly when the novelty was worn off. This was Jill's most bitter pill of realisation. She knew now that the impulse that had driven her to build Firstlings had been a mere girlish whim, and also that despite all she had said that she had really felt all the time a little philanthropic air of superiority towards the mothers.

In those sleepless nights, Jill had been honest with herself. She was tired of the Tired Mothers. She wanted petting and caring for herself. She was not a big soul, but a little one, often tired, and too unsaint-like for her many responsibilities. She was like the mother of nineteen, wanting to be taken into custody, out of the struggling amongst the anxieties of life.

Firstlings was not built upon a rock. It had been built out of a feeling of pique that she had been jilted, it had been an indirect way of proving herself a martyr and a saint, as compared with Harry. Firstlings was bruit out of sorrow, not out of joy; out of philanthropy, not fellowship; out of pity allied to scorn, loving as it was.

Worst disillusionment of all, Jill had set herself to build Firstlings to *please herself*, not to help the mothers. It had been a toy to her. She cringed inwardly as she walked away, suffering that worst disappointment, disappointment in herself, feeling a dishonest wretch. But in reality she was too hard on herself. Jill had been quite sincere in her desire to help humanity. She had done a good thing from a wrong motive, it is true. Her gradual weariness had come as much as anything from the incapacity of her youth to deal with the problems facing her, and the perception that she was not able to touch a fringe of even the sordid miseries of London. She was merely giving a holiday once a year to a handful of tired mothers out of the world's millions, and already she had received one or two letters which plainly showed, between the lines, that the glimpse of beauty the writers had had at Firstlings had aggravated their sense of hardship and wrong in the pinched homes they had gone back to.

"Somebody ought to be hung for it," thought Jill, vehemently. "There ought not to be any tired mothers in the first place. It's all wrong somehow. Anyhow, *I* can't help it."

Musing thus, she walked into a poppy-proud dowager, powdered to the hair, and further made hideous by a purple veil with a huge spot that came over one eye.

"Oh, I'm so sorry!" gasped Jill, blushing.

The poppy-proud lady was very annoyed, and muttered something. Jill felt considerably like laughing for a moment, just as the gawky lads laughed in Breezeton lanes if they banged into anyone.

"I really ought to look where I'm going, though," thought Jill, and roused herself to what was going about her.

It was raining faster. She put up the mushroom of an umbrella, with the handle which the mother of eight had said was real pearl, on presenting it to her, on behalf of the rest of the mothers, the first lot of mothers who had drifted through Firstlings.

"Drip—drip," said the rain on the umbrella-top.

Jill was cuddling the handle. The mothers had given it to her.

Even though she had opened a door leading out of all that greyness just for a whim, and though she knew that it not only led out of it but back into it, Jill was sure of one vital thing. She had no right to slam the door of Firstlings on tired faces. The first enthusiasm had dropped away from her, leaving her without wings. She was a tired mother herself. But—she must go on. There was no turning back.

That was the one great ideal that came to Jill, in this despairing realisation of her own failings. She must strive to keep Firstlings going, even though it did not seem to matter to her, and she must keep it going on the same high lines as those on which it had begun.

She was nearing the vicinity of the square where dwelt the millionaire she had come to beg, borrow or steal from, when she had reached this clear decision. There were no shops here. The selectness of the neighbourhood made itself felt. The houses had a stately but somewhat dreary look, and Jill compared them, to their disadvantage, with the little house where Mandy and Giles had lived, with the bush of lad's love by the door, and the white gate latching loosely on a garden where the grey of the lavender spikes went so gloriously with the flush of the rambling roses. Jill was beginning to feel a little nervous. She got the ridiculous notion that the houses were faces, grave faces, the windows—lorgnettes, and this roused her sense of humour. She tried to think out her case, but the pit-pit of the raindrops on her umbrella distracted her. She wondered what effect the sight of her card would have on a stranger.

JILL BENNETT,
Firstlings House for Tired Mothers,
Breezeton, Yorks.

She saw the card in a mental vision, carried on a silver tray to the millionaire. She assumed, of course, in her quixotic way, that millionaires were mostly in. The nearer she got to No. 63 the more certain she became that she should never gain admittance, the less like Dick Turpin she felt, and the nearer akin to a beggar—which surprised her.

"Oh, do you mind my coming under your umbrella?" came a charming voice at Jill's side.

"Do," cried Jill, bobbing the mushroom umbrella over the head of a gaily dressed girl, a girl most unsuitably dressed for the outside grey, or so it seemed.

"Lord, how it rains," said the girl. "The rain it raineth every day," she chirruped. Jill guessed at once that the girl was on the stage. She had a close look at her as they came under an arc lamp.

"My double!" laughed the smart girl, gazing back at Jill, incredulously.

"I've seen you in my looking glass often," Jill acknowledged quickly.

"We—it's quite bewildering," confessed the girl. They walked on, the smart girl talking all the while.

When they had passed the ninth rain-blurred street lamp, Jill knew almost all there was to know about Daisy Keith, even her name. Jill was not surprised. In her short life she had been the recipient of many confidences, from so varied a source as shrimp-sellers and insurance agents. The girl was evidently one of those whom Mandy would have described as putting all in the window they had in the shop. There was a certain naive freshness about her, though.

"But—" said Jill, sharply, the mushroom umbrella letting the raindrops fall on the girl's hat.

"Oh, yes. I know all about it," the girl said mockingly, "but I'm on my last quid, and no prospect of a part— and if my clothes get jiggered up—oh Lord, I can't go on any longer. I can't, I tell you. I've gone straight up to now, but there's nothing to it. You should see the boxes of Madonna lilies and chocs I keep getting! The chocs just help to vary the diet of toast and marmalade, and keep me from getting too thin. It's fatal for a chorus girl to get thin, you know—or at least, you don't know. Well, as I said, he's a millionaire. When you get taken up by a millionaire, it's all plain sailing, so I'm going to keep my appointment. It said in the paper he had a chill. That's all my eye. He's waiting for me. Fancy a millionaire pacing the room and looking at the clock—waiting for a girl who has only earned enough to keep body and soul together! Oh, yes, I'm going."

This was said most defiantly.

"You're not," said Jill.

"Oh, yes—" laughed Daisy.

"I won't let you," said Jill, and seized the girl's arm. Daisy tried to shake her off, whilst Jill searched rapidly for the right word.

"Think of your mother—" she said.

"Oh, ma'll be delighted!" said Daisy. "She has often reproached me for not making use of my chances. You see, there was Daniel—Dan's my cousin. We were rather gone on each other. He went out East to make good, but I haven't heard for a year. He must have gone under, or he'd have written. So—I can't go on any longer. It's the last straw that breaks the camel's back."

She was speaking now without that miserable attempt to make believe that she did not care for anything.

"But—you're not a camel," asserted Jill.

Daisy Keith stared at the girl who was holding her arm. Then she had to laugh. That remark of Jill's was too funny. A warm, human sense of fellowship sprung up in the heart of the little dancer.

"Will twenty pounds be any good to you—until you get work?" queried Jill, smiling herself.

Daisy Keith experienced a rapid revulsion of feeling. She stared at Jill, the while Jill unselfishly guarded her hat with the mushroom umbrella, whilst the drippings trickled upon Jill's own headgear, the roses of which had reminded the dancer all the time of—Daniel and herself in a summer garden—before he went East.

The revulsion was too much. Daisy leaned against the lamp-post, and cried like a little child. It was over in half a minute.

"You'll think I'm a cry-baby," she said, smiling shamefacedly.

"I don't think it's any credit to anyone not to be able to feel," said Jill.

She gave Daisy her card, and asked her to call at Halgrove Chambers in the morning.

Jill stood with Daisy's own card in her hand, watching the mist swallow up the unsuitably garbed figure. Then—drawing a deep breath, she slipped the wet card into her bag. She had just remembered that by telling Daisy to call at Halgrove Chambers she would have to go there herself, and would run the risk of meeting Mason.

She moved forwards in the direction Daisy had taken. Was it any good going to call on a libertine on behalf of tired mothers? And if it were, could any good come of it? That was what Jill was thinking. She could not make up her mind. As Mandy would have said, she had a mind but wanted someone to make it up for her.

"If there are seven or less lamp-posts up to the door 63 I'll try," Jill said to herself. "If there are more, I'll not."

She walked along counting the lamp-posts. She saw them dimly through the mist, and as she walked her mind was mixed up between Daisy Keith, Will Mason, the tired mothers and the millionaire.

There were just seven lamp-posts. The seventh was right in front of 63.

Her knees shook as she went up the steps, and when the bell rang its echoes shook her nerves, and she wanted to run away, just as she had once done when ringing the bell of a dentist when first she came to London. The echoes died away. The door swung open and Jill saw a light-flooded hall, that was like a long panel of rich colour opening out of the grey mist.

"Can I see Mr. Gilly Minton?" inquired Jill. The expression on the footman's face was really very scaring to a person of Jill's simplicity.

"Have you an appointment, madam?" he asked.

Jill made up her mind more rapidly than ever she had done in her life.

"Oh, yes," she smiled, and began fumbling in her bag. She had perceived that no one without an appointment would get to see Mr. Minton. Before she had time to realise her own daring she was following the silk-stockinged footman to whom she had given her card—the card given to her by little Daisy Keith. Evidently the footman had been told to admit her.

The awful solemnity of the other footman at the end of the hall, who came forward with wooden steps and took her dripping umbrella, his face showing no sign of animation, made Jill want to laugh and scream. Already she was half repenting her rashness.

"This way, madam," said the other, leading her into a little room. They passed through this and along a yellow passage with a black door set midway in the wall.

"Miss Keith, sir," announced the footman, monotonously, and Jill was ushered into a yellow room, with black furniture, and touches of orange from chrysanthemums in silver vases. A great fire on the yellow and black tiled hearthstone showed up a black settee where a young man was reclining, his pale face and jet-black hair having the background of a bronze-gold cushion.

"Come in, Daisy," he said without rising from the settee. "You can go, James."

James went.

"Sit down," said the man on the settee.

Jill sat down. She was glad to be able to do so, for her knees were shaking under her.

Ting-ting, went the telephone bell.

"No rest for the wicked," smiled the young man languidly, and rose with a langour that made Jill want to shake him.

"Hello," he called. Then, "Tell her to go to bed. Best thing for the flu."

Another silence.

"Oh, yes. I'm better," he called again. "Give her some whisky, good and hot. Goodbye."

It was only as he stumbled in recrossing to the settee that Jill saw, with horror, that he was drunk. She became paralysed with fear.

"So—you've come, Daisy, Daisy—" he said, looking at her intently.

Jill nodded.

"Not got a part yet?" he asked.

As he swayed a little, his hands in his pockets, his black eyes expressing sympathy, a very fine sympathy, Jill lost some of her fear. She shook her head.

"Poor little girl," he said. "Been there myself, Daisy. Been there—myself. I say, you look different, Daisy— and you're sure you've not got the flu, old girl? You look so white."

He leaned on the back of her chair. Jill could believe that she looked white. She felt white, as Giles used to say, thinking it a glorious bit of wit.

"Come to make the great sacrifice, eh?" said Minton, touching Jill's cheek, tenderly.

Jill sprang out of her chair as though the touch set an automatic spring in action, which flung her out of her sitting position.

Minton surveyed the white indignation of her face.

"Look here, Daisy," he said, swaying towards her——

"I'm not Daisy," said Jill, almost terrified out of her senses.

Minton surveyed her.

"Then who the devil are you?" he asked, in great amazement.

"I'm Jill Bennett," said Jill, striving after regality, with as much success as she had striven for privacy at Firstlings. "I've called on behalf of the tired mothers. You are very rich. I thought you would perhaps like to give back to the poor some of the money you have ground out of them," said Jill. "At least it would be something for you to remember when dying."

The Dick Turpin-like attitude of mind had come back to Jill.

"Daisy!" said Minton, clapping his hands. "Bravo, Daisy! Daisy, you've genius. I wasn't sure of it, but I am now. Daisy, some more."

Jill surveyed him, the anger rising in her.

"If you would care to contribute to my mothers, you have your opportunity," she said, quietly.

Minton flung himself into a chair at this, and laughed until the tears ran down his cheeks.

"Daisy!" he gasped. "Cut it out, Daisy, I'll get you a part. It's fine, Daisy."

Jill began to wonder how to prove to him that she really was Jill Bennett.

"How many mothers did you say you had, Daisy? I know you could have forefathers, but I'd no idea you could have more than one mother. Tired, did you say they were? Well, what do you want to do for them?"

"I really am Jill Bennett, a Yorkshire woman by birth," said Jill, going up to Minton, "and I have a Guest House for tired mothers. If you could give only a thousand pounds, I should be gratified on their account; otherwise, the House will have to close."

Minton unexpectedly seized Jill's hand in his. She gave a faint, terrified scream, looking at him fiercely.

Minton was gazing down at Jill's hand.

"Daisy had a scar," he muttered. "There's none here, and yet—I say, Daisy, have I got the rats? You know, those things that make you see pink monkeys and white mice?"

It was evidently no use talking to him. Jill got her hand back, very glad to do so, and did attempt an explanation, which he said he understood, but which she was sure he did not.

"Have I got the rats?" he asked at intervals.

"Will you please write that I may see you to-morrow?" queried Jill, persistently. "And say that I am Jill Bennett?"

She had quite ceased to fear him now, for one thing was quite plain to her—he was not a cinema millionaire blackguard. She really began to doubt if he had meant any ill to Daisy.

When Jill went away she had a note, which said, simply:—
Admit Jill Bennett, to see me to-morrow, at ten a.m.
G. M.

Thus ended Jill's interview with G. Minton. She left him pouring out another glass of whisky and soda, and asking James, the wooden-faced one, if he thought he had the rats, as Daisy had said she was not Daisy and had started a Home for Tired Washerwomen. Jill ran down the stone steps. When she reached the first lamp-post she leaned against it—and laughed and laughed and laughed and nearly got locked up. A policeman followed her several hundred yards.

"I wonder what the rats are like," she mused.

She unfolded Gilly Minton's permit for the morrow, in the train, and re-read it, then decided to tuck it in her purse rather than the bag. She opened the purse. She missed something. A look of horror stole over her face.

"Have you lost something?" queried a voice, sympathetically. Jill was staggered. Sympathy on a tube-railway was as odd as her millionaire. The woman who had spoken to her was a fat Cockney, and her breath smelled of whisky, too.

"No—yes—that is—" faltered Jill.

Quite suddenly, she actually began to laugh, to shake with laughter, in the tube train full of Londoners. It was too awful. She could not stop laughing, so stared out through the window, swallowing down laughter, choking with it.

She had given the starchy James, the footman, not a sovereign, as she had fancied, but a button, a brass button, from one of Giles' old coats, which she had kept for a mascot.

She stepped out without looking at anyone. She knew they thought her mad, all those serious-faced people sitting two by two, facing each other, silent, cut off from each other. She had not dared to look at them again because their serious faces would have made her laugh more, she knew. She had a pain in her side with laughing, as she walked along the sub-way, and hailed a taxi going towards Halgrove Chambers. She went up the stairs. All was dark, silent. Mason must have gone off again, and the caretaker was out. She shook again with laughter at the recollection of the brass button with the anchor on it. She laughed her way up the stairs, glad to let out that laughter she had had to choke down in the train.

It was just as she stood on the little green mat, still laughing, that a door opened, letting out a dull gleam of firelight.

"Hello!" came a startled voice. "Something the matter, Jill?"

It was Mason. He had been sitting in the firelight.

Mason made Jill want to laugh more than ever.

"Oh no," she said, politely, "nothing whatever. I think I must have got the rats, whatever those are."

She went inside, switched on the light, and Mason heard the key turn in the lock.

"Jill!" he said, in alarm, at this unusual behaviour. "Jill! At least assure me that you have not been drinking."

Laughter, a perfect peal of it, came from Jill, on the other side of the door.

"What are the rats?" he heard at last.

"It means—delirium tremens," he said. "Jill—something is the matter with you. Let me in. I'll only stay five minutes."

"I'm all right," said Jill, naturally. "I'm not drunk. What an idea! But—I say—I've given a m—millionaire's footman a—a—br—brass button."

She began to laugh again.

"Let me come in. Tell me about it," coaxed Mason.

He was quite sure, now, that Jill was going mad, or suffering brain fever or something else as awful. But Jill was adamant.

It was some time after, in his stockinged-feet that he crept towards that door, knelt down softly, and looked through the keyhole. It framed Jill, Jill pale and tired-looking, but quite sane, contentedly sipping a cup of tea. He drew a deep breath of relief and stole away.

Whatever could have made her laugh like that, he mused, and talk about having the rats, and about millionaires and brass buttons.

Anyhow, she was all right now. The sight of her had reassured him.

He went to bed, but not to sleep. He did not pretend that Jill should steal away again, and he wanted to know why she had so laughed. Which was just what Jill wondered as she brushed her hair before the glass, next morning. The pain at the nape of her neck was terrible this morning.

CHAPTER XVIII

MASON TRIES AGAIN

"Let me cook the breakfast," said Mason, masterfully.

Jill gave in with as good a grace as she could muster.

"No. You can't make tea," she told him. "I can make tea."

An embarrassing feeling of domesticity invaded the couple. Jill stole a glance at Mason as he cautiously lowered the egg-poacher into the pan of boiling water. He had rolled up his shirt sleeves, was without a jacket, and looked very much at home, as he knelt on the curb.

"Those will be O.K.," he said, with an air of contentment, looking up at Jill, who was measuring out tea from the Chinese canister.

Jill was afraid that he would begin to ask her to marry him again. But he did not. Breakfast was soon ready. Jill sat at one end of the long table, and he sat at the other, discussing all sorts of small things in between the courtesies of the breakfast-table.

"How are the mothers going on?" he asked, unexpectedly.

Jill gave him little pictures of the mothers. He watched her keenly. She endeavoured to put more enthusiasm into her manner.

"How will you keep Firstlings going?" he asked. Jill started.

"Oh, Mr. Wicks told me," he said. "That was why you came up to London to marry somebody old enough to be your grandfather, I presume."

Jill took refuge in silence.

"Salt?" queried he.

Jill nodded, and watched the salt pot pushed half the length of the table and leaned over to reach it.

"You will have to rely on subscribers," said Mason. "And you will get all the wrong subscribers, because you will be so serious, and appealing, and they will get no limelight."

Jill bristled.

"I have an appointment this morning," she said, "and hope to get five thousand pounds for the mothers. Anyhow, Firstlings is not faced with closing down immediately. I've put the thing in pawn. We can go on two years."

Mason stirred his tea round and round.

"You can't," he said sympathetically.

"We can," said Jill, doggedly.

"Oh—Wicks told me about it," he said. "You gave his name as your legal adviser, didn't you? Well, the executors of the solicitor who loaned you the money on Firstlings have written Mr. Wicks."

"The executors?" asked Jill, in amazement.

"The poor old chap's dead," said Mason. "His affairs are all anyhow. They want the five hundred pounds refunding at the earliest convenience,—within a month, or—I'm afraid they are going to sell the furniture."

Jill turned very white.

But she went on eating her egg.

"Let me help you, Jill," said Mason, eagerly. "Look here, I'm not without money, for I don't fling it about like you do, and—really, you must let me help. I've got stakes in Firstlings. I built the place. Don't you see? I'm a sort of father to it. It's a sort of baby of mine, too. I've eight hundred pounds I don't really need."

"No—" said Jill.

She said it in a choking sort of way.

"Why?" queried Mason, with the look that had made the lion roar in his eyes.

"Because I won't," said Jill.

"Because it's a sort of tradition that a woman should not accept help from a man who is in love with her," said Mason, cheerfully scoffing. "As if that is not the best kind of reason when it's the best sort of love."

"I can't have you losing money by Firstlings," said Jill.

"But I have lost money by Firstlings," said Mason, cheerfully. "I lost five hundred pounds by building Firstlings, and my heart, Jill—my whole heart."

"You lost—" gasped Jill.

"I under estimated the cost," said Mason. "How worried you are over that five hundred pounds, Jill, and not in the least upset about my poor heart."

Jill took another piece of toast.

"Look here," said Jill, despairingly, leaning her chin on her hand, "what would you do?"

"I should marry me," said Mason, calmly.

"I mean about the furniture," said Jill. "And I can't refund the five hundred pounds. I've only a hundred— and some of that is spoken for."

"But you said you could raise five thousand," began Mason.

Just then the bell rang.

"Oh, I'll get the papers—" he said and darted out of the room. He tossed one to Jill, on sitting down again. But Jill had not the heart to read the paper. She ate mechanically, thinking of Firstlings, that was to have gone for ever, closing in four short weeks, the wonder, the talk, the laughter there would be in the Press.

Her eyes stared unseeingly at the pictures on the paper beside her plate. Mason was reading the headings, the only things he did read, unless the Irish question was up.

A short exclamation from Jill made him look up. She pushed the paper across to him in answer to his surprise. Her eyes were quite wild and her hand had ruffled her hair as though she had a grievance against it.

"Left-hand corner—bogus millionaire!" groaned Jill. "Oh, I couldn't have believed anything like this could happen out of a farce! I went begging from him and he's only an impostor—valet to the real millionaire. I want to scream."

"Scream then," said Mason, smiling.

Jill looked across at his face with its cheerful sympathy.

Tears welled up in her eyes and before she knew what to do, Mason was by her chair and wiping her face with his handkerchief.

"Look here," he said, "I'll tell you what I'll do. I'll pull this thing round for you before I sail. There! That's a promise. Cheer up. But now—what is your unreasonable objection to marrying me? I'm sure I'm a nice fellow."

His mock air of conceit made Jill smile. But there was something pathetic about it too.

"Tell me—Jill," he said.

Jill wavered.

Did it really matter that her uncle had made a bargain on their behalf, or that she would have to tell Mason that she had not buried her sweetheart but had been jilted by him?

"Jill " pleaded Mason.

Her name was too much like the word "jilted."

"I couldn't tell him I'd been thrown over," said the inner Jill. She had gone quite sick at the thought of having to tell him and veered away from it with great relief.

"I—I don't care for you," said Jill, her face turned away.

"If you let me go away," said Mason, suddenly older and grimmer than Jill could have imagined him, "I shall never come back. I shall know that you don't care. Now—about Firstlings—"

In twenty minutes Mason had placed the position of Firstlings before Jill, and Jill—Jill had said she would let him help to pull Firstlings round, because of the right he had. He had built it and had lost five hundred pounds.

"Now, I shan't worry you any more about us," said Mason. "But I'd like to go to Kensington Gardens with you. I shall have to be off to-day. I'm spending the rest of my time in Devon, after the Firstlings business is over. But I'd so like us to go to Kensington Gardens, Jill. Look on it as a last request."

He grinned cheerfully enough, but his face was pale under the tan and his eyes had a worried look.

Jill promised, and Mason went to his own rooms. Daisy Keith came a quarter of an hour later.

"Have you seen the paper?" was her first question.

Jill nodded.

They gazed at each other—and Jill's smile made Daisy burst into laughter.

"Only a bogus millionaire, too," said Daisy. "Well!"

A moment's silence followed.

"And to think," she went on, "it was so near the turn of the tide, too. I've heard from Dan, this morning, and he will soon be able to send for me. Also—I've to call and see Gallagher Thomas, who is producing "Fairy Bells" and—oh, you dear little thing. You've turned my luck."

Jill had great difficulty in making Daisy accept the loan of two pounds, so sure was she of getting on in the "Fairy Bells" revue. Jill gave her the Breezeton address and said she should like to hear how she had gone on. So they parted. It was certainly another creature who danced down the staircase compared with that which Jill had encountered the previous night.

Mason was waiting for Jill at eleven o'clock. She met him on the stairs and without a word they proceeded into the streets.

The spell of the old square, with its echoes, fell upon them.

"I had thought to live here for years and years," laughed Mason, "and to grow as famous as my master. But soon I shall be studying mosques, blue cupolas, and gilded fanes. I like best the quiet silver-grey of English architecture, though."

Jill was silent. With Mason she had never experienced that constraint to chatter, nor been thought unfriendly. She could dare to be silent with him.

Then he told her about his mother, how from his childhood she had encouraged his bent for drawing—how, when she was left widowed and poor, she had lived almost meanly that he might be placed with a good draughtsman.

"To her I owe everything," he said—"everything."

Jill felt as guilty as a criminal. Away in Devon was a little woman with grey hair, who had sacrificed all for her son, and she, Jill Bennett, was driving him out of the country because she did not dare confess that she had once been jilted—and because of natural perversions—because someone had "made it worth while" for them to marry each other.

"I will try to tell him," thought Jill, with a beating heart.

They entered Kensington Gardens just at the hour when it was being deserted.

"The Daphne bushes smell glorious in the spring," said Mason, musingly. Then, he added, "Which way now?"

"We'll have a look at Peter," suggested Jill.

"I wonder if the kids have lost as much as they have gained in Peter being materialised," said Mason. "Peter was a thing of dream. They imagined him flying over here, but now—they may touch him, and he stands here all day, without moving."

"It was Peter who aided and abetted me in building Firstlings," said Jill. "You see—I came here, often,—just when I was in trouble. The daffodils were just out. And I saw the other sort of mothers, you know,—well-fed, well-dressed—"

"The sort of mother you would be if you should marry me," said Mason.

"No—" said Jill, determinedly. "Not the sort I should be. At least—I should like to do more than bask in the sunshine. Do you know—my grandfather was shot in Peterloo? I am going to find out *why* there is poverty,—why there is need for Rest Houses for Tired Mothers."

"Well, how did Peter inveigle you into being a philanthropist?" asked Mason, lightly. He was staring at the mound where the daffodils would soon dance. As an artist he admired the bronze figure, so childlike and easy, with its flute in its hand, and the beautiful base with the hares and mice and birds and fairies and angels, so loved by the children. Jill and he sat down.

"No, not a philanthropist," denied Jill, wincing. "At least I did not mean to be. Well, I went to Bow and Poplar and—saw the mothers and children there, the children who know at five years of age that cocoa is dearer than tea!—the children who are never young once, never mind never growing up! I—seemed to carry Peter in my mind's eye, all the time, with the daffodils round him, in this green place,—and—*the other* children, and—I wanted to do something for the women. So—I got the idea. You see I was in great trouble—"

Jill felt that someone was pouring cold water down her back. She was trying to approach the subject—to confess that she had been jilted, that all that story of burying her sweetheart was a lie, a lie to save her own pride.

She met Mason's gaze.

It disturbed her intention to make a clean breast of the whole business. She grew afraid of him. She had used to care about Harry Thorn's opinion about her dress. She felt that it would be like death to acknowledge that she had lied, lied to Mandy and Giles, lied to him, just to save her pride. It never struck her that Will Mason might see the funny side of burying someone who was not dead—or that in any case, whatever she had done, he would overlook it. Jill was only awed by the bigness of the man, his scrupulous honesty, his plain frankness. It was such a poor reason she had to give for all that deceit. "I was afraid to let people know—that a man had changed his mind—that I wasn't so priceless as I had fancied." Mason, in his brief friendship, had gradually been making Jill ashamed of this fear of hers,—this little pride. Gradually, very gradually, it is true. On the last time she had seen Harry, for the first time since he had jilted her, she had felt no Irish resentment against what had been his unutterable meanness.

Jill's shame had changed. She was now afraid of confessing that she had been so silly as to tell indirect lies, to prove Harry dead, rather than faithless.

"You were saying you were in trouble at the time," said Mason. Jill started. She had been staring out beyond Peter Pan, forgetful that she had broken off midway in a sentence.

"You mean when you buried your sweetheart, I presume?" inquired Mason. There was a small repressed smile on that side of his face which was out of Jill's sight. They were both conscious of the half yard of space dividing them, as they sat on the little rustic bench.

Jill nodded.

"The fact is—" she began.

She tried to make her tongue say "I did not bury him"—but it would not.

"It was a great blow to me," she went on, and could have screamed because instead of making a clean breast of it, she was sinking deeper into the mire.

"So you thought you would devote your life to Tired Mothers," finished Mason.

Jill nodded.

She gave up the conflict. She was more afraid of Mason knowing the extent of her silliness than she was of his going away. It paralysed her to think of how he would change, how he would show his disappointment that she could lie as she had lied.

"You look cold," said Mason, solicitously. "You are shivering. We'll go and have lunch. I say—we'll lunch in Soho, at one of those jolly Bohemian places."

Thus ended Jill's attempt to break down the barrier that kept her from giving way to Mason's plea that she marry him. She could not marry him with the lie on her conscience, a lie without any other extenuating excuse other than that she could not bear anyone to know she had been jilted. She could not tell him the truth—for fear of losing his good opinion. Jill was drifting now.

They went to Soho, and had lunch in a jolly little French place, with canary cages hung from the roof. Blue-overalled workmen came in, mixing up with artists, artists' models, ministers of the gospel (come for experience) and at the next table to the couple sat a negro pugilist, in the finest of fine cloth.

"Do you think those two people are married?" asked Jill.

Mason looked.

"Yes," he said. "But not to each other."

"There are people like that," said Jill, musingly. "I have a fickle nature, though you might not think it."

She was making another desperate effort to get round to the subject of Harry, whom she had so soon been glad to be free from.

"You," said Mason, with a smile. "See, this is my waiter. Observe his fine presence. An Englishman could not serve with such dignity. This dinner, Jill, will cost one shilling. It is worth it to look at Henri. Shall we have herring after soup? I never tasted such herrings."

Jill was beginning to feel more frivolous than ever she had done in her life. There was a genial gaiety about this place to which she was responding. Though it is quite true that she would not have dared to be there without Mason.

"Potatoe soup," decided Jill.

"Henri, we will have potatoe soup," said Mason. Henri bowed, it was almost imperceptible, but he bowed.

"I have never seen him smile," said Mason.

"Gilly Minton's footmen did not smile," said Jill, "but dignified English serfs only looked foolish. The French are wonderful people."

She was watching Henri, napkin on arm, walking up the long room, with the beaded curtains screening it from view of the passers- by.

"We will send him out for some Harvest Burgundy," Mason said, dreamily, as Henri approached.

"Wine?" asked Jill.

"Oh, it's just Harvest Burgundy. You couldn't get the rats off that. " Mason answered. "I wonder what you would be like, Jill, if you were drunk."

Jill smiled at the meditativeness on Mason's face. He was trying to pretend he was one of the smart set. It was the funniest thing she had ever seen.

"I was once drunk,"—said Jill, gravely.

The one who had been trying to shock was shocked.

Henri arrived at the little table.

"Let me tell you of the effect," said Jill, taking up her soup-spoon, when Henri went away, "never mind the cause. Let it suffice that I was in dreadful trouble."

"Jill, come outside. I want to talk to you. Do you mean to say that you have been drunk?" half groaned Mason. There was a perfect babble of voices in the room, parsons discussing Theology, an artist pulling another artist's colour scheme to pieces to his own model, the pugilist airing his views on whether Jack Johnson would win in the next fight. No one could hear Mason.

Jill laughed.

"I was told that I sang, danced, and made original poetry," she said gaily. "I was told that tea was wasted on me, and that I ought I to drink whisky. You see, I was in great trouble—having the flu and being compelled to go to the office next day so I was desperate. Three pennyworth of real Irish and the juice of a lemon turned me into a Gaelic prophetess and seer, and then—Mrs. Greenwall carried me to bed.——But—it did not cure the flu."

"You little wretch!" said Mason.

Jill had really given him a shock, until she told him about the illness.

"Shall we try the herrings?" queried Jill.

They did. Jill was astonished at common herrings tasting like that.

"I'd like the mothers to taste them," she said, in much the same spirit that the mother of nineteen would have said she wondered what the baby would think of raspberry jam.

"We'll ask Henri to tell us how they are made," said Mason.

"Oh, don't ask for recipes when we've only paid a shilling for the dinner"—gasped Jill. Henri was coming towards them, with meat, potatoes, and pickled fruit.

"Henri," said Mason, "this lady would like to know how those herrings get their delightful flavour."

Henri took his napkin from one arm, and placed it upon the other. The grave dignity of his personality became a more wonderful thing than ever. He looked at Jill, who was looking at him. She was very unlike anyone who came to the restaurant, and he saw all kinds of people.

"Those, madam," he said in broken English, "are herrings who have passed the night with onions."

"Thanks, so much," said Jill, looking up at Henri.

Henri smiled as much as to say that he would have given away the whole secrets of the menu to Jill. He walked away, covered with grave dignity once more.

"That was a triumph, Jill," said Mason. "Henri smiled."

"You did not send him out for the Harvest Burgundy," said Jill.

"Afraid of the consequences," said Mason. "If threepenny-worth of whisky would turn you into a Gaelic prophetess, what would be the result of a half-bottle of Harvest Burgundy?"

Black coffee, bread and cheese arrived and the royal meal was almost over. As they drank the black coffee, Jill had never looked so delightful. Henri had just turned his back.

"Jill—" began Mason, and paused.

One of the absolute dead silences that are lulls in the conversation, happened, and the whole establishment heard Mason say, beseechingly, "Will you marry me?"

It was like a thunderbolt dropping in the place. Jill thought that Mason had done it purposely. She went quite white at this publicity, and said distinctly, "Certainly not. Please pass me the sugar."

Jill never knew how they managed to escape.

"I'm awfully sorry—Jill," said Mason, as they were closing the door.

Jill was more than indignant. She believed he had tried coercion, as a last resort.

"I will never ask you again," promised Mason. "I really don't know why I continue to make such a complete ass of myself."

He saw Jill off in the train that was going north, and handed her in another of the thick pots, full of tea, just as he had done when he saw her off before.

"Give my love to the mothers," he said.

They both looked absurdly young.

Jill did not even lean out of the window as the train moved.

"Good-bye, Jill," called Mason.

"Good-bye," said Jill, firmly.

The train gathered speed, and Jill leaned back against the cushions. She was going back to Breezeton, and the Mothers. Mason had gone out of her life—for ever.

CHAPTER XIX

BACK AT FIRSTLINGS

Janet Burns opened the door in answer to Jill's ringing. It was just seven in the morning, and all was shadowy, but Jill saw that the snow was cleared away. "How tired you must be," said Janet. The rest of the mothers were not up, so Jill took breakfast with Janet. Jill tried to feel glad that she was back. Later, as she was sitting in the little blue room there came a tap at the door.

"Come in," said Jill.

Mrs. Williams entered.

"Janet said you were back," she said, "and I couldn't help wondering how you had got on with the millionaire."

"He was a bogus millionaire," said Jill, and told Mrs. Williams the story, briefly. She told her also of the decease of the lawyer who had loaned the money on Firstlings.

"We are at the end of our tether," said Jill. "In a month Firstlings will close, unless—something turns up." She laughed wearily at the Micawber-like phrase.

"If the funds do come, I want to hand over the management to you," said Jill, suddenly. "I'm not fit to be—a Mother. I'm not. It has just been a whim. If the funds don't turn up,—well, I'll stick the storm. But, if they do, I want you to be the Mother. Will you?"

Mrs. Williams lit up.

"I've been wanting to be a mother all my life," she said. "I daresay David could get work at the brick factory."

The next four days brought no letter from Mason. He was keeping his promise. But Daisy Keith wrote, enclosing two pounds, and saying Jill had turned her luck, and that her first appearance in "Fairy Bells" had been a stunning success. There was also a card from Geoffrey Barnes—a card with the picture of an ocean liner on it, Jill was glad that these two people were faring better—glad in a tired sort of way.

"I wonder if I caught the flu from Gilly Minton," she would muse. She was really feeling ill. Whilst every morning was the thought—another day off the number that stand between him and sailing.

"Only a few more days, and he will be off," thought Jill, pulling on her stockings one morning. "I wish the beastly weather would mend."

It had rained for three days. Jill blamed her deepening sense of depression on that.

That morning came a letter from—Gilly Minton, the real Gilly Minton. It contained astonishing news. He was coming down to see Firstlings. Jill could hardly believe it. She ran into Mrs. Williams' bedroom with the letter, and Mrs. Williams jumped up from one of her exercises for strengthening the waist muscles.

"What do you think we are having to dinner?" said Jill.

Mrs. Williams shook her head.

"A millionaire," answered Jill.

Mrs. Williams stared at the sudden apparition of a joyous Jill.

"We are out of the wood, out of the wood," laughed Jill. "Oh, what a relief! It's been an awful worry."

She cried, sitting on Mrs. Williams' bed.

"You will tell the mothers, now, I suppose," said Mrs. Williams.

"That a millionaire is coming?" queried Jill. "No, indeed. They would not be themselves at all."

"Come with me to the station," begged Jill.

Mrs. Williams went.

The real Mr. Gilly Minton, looking out of the train window, recognised Jill, also Mrs. Williams. They walked along to Firstlings, with the sun shining down on the rain-pools in the lanes, and everything looking its best.

Mr. Minton interviewed Jill in the little blue room sitting on the chair Mandy had used to occupy. Jill did not feel at all like Dick Turpin, now.

"What decided you to come?" queried Jill.

"These," said Minton.

He opened his valise, and took out a sheaf of drawings and water colour sketches,—and there Jill saw herself, and Janet Burns, and Mrs. Williams, and the mother of eight, and the mother of nineteen—all so wonderfully delineated, with little odd sketches of corners of Firstlings, the hall, the garden, the way the grounds looked on a misty morning.

"Your friend, Mr. Mason, sent these to me," he said. "He is quite a genius. How much will keep the place going?"

Jill did not want to ask too much, neither did she want to ask too little. It was funny to Mr. Minton to see her.

"Will ten thousand pounds be enough?" he asked.

Jill flushed.

"You darling!" she exclaimed.

Mr. Minton blushed at that. He was quite a young man, though Jill had not seemed to realise it. Jill was the prettiest English girl he had seen—and the most natural.

"On one condition," he said.

Jill looked anxious.

Was he going to want publicity and lime-light. According to Jill's idea that would ruin the place.

"The gift is anonymous," he said. "You see, I should be pulled out of the place with begging letters, and—I am not an indiscriminate giver."

"Then you think—" began Jill.

"I think that if you could give all you had, I can give ten thousand," said Minton. He evidently knew the whole story.

They went in to dinner, after this. Mrs. Williams had told the mothers that a gentleman from London was come to see the place. There was no suspicion that a millionaire sat at table. The Burnley woman innocently discussed politics with him, and told him that in her opinion a revolution was coming, and the sooner it came the better, for she was fed up at the idea of going back on margarine again. She also showed him the photograph of her husband.

"Allus workin', he is," said Mrs. Robinson. "An' what better are we? There's only threepence difference between them as works an' them as plays, an' them as plays 'as it!"

Minton caught Jill's gaze—and gave her a gentle, smiling look. It was evident that he enjoyed himself immensely. He stayed to the evening entertainment— the first part of it, and heard Mrs. Robinson sing, "We'd better bide a wee"—but when Mrs. Williams sang in Welsh he looked as though he thought he was amply repaid for his gift in that alone.

Jill took him to the station.

It felt queer to be walking with a millionaire. The mist was falling. The hills were magnified by it, and stood like giant sorrows, brooding, so it seemed to Jill. The station lights looked tearful through the mist.

"I suppose she was right," said Gilly Minton, musingly.

Jill glanced askance at him.

"The woman who spoke of the Revolution," said Gilly Minton. "I think it is coming. Of course, we shall ward it off as long as possible, and my hands will have to be unclenched from my possessions. Still—I think she was right. I should go mad if I had to lead lives like they have. All the same—one cannot help taking sides. I wonder which side you will be on."

Jill looked at him.

"The winning side," she said coolly.

"Oh, opportunist?" he suggested, laughingly.

*The winning side," repeated Jill. "Can you wonder which that will be?"

He gave a little start.

"Oh, I see—" he said, gravely.

"When they once realise all they have missed," said Jill.

"We shall catch it," he said, laughing.

They had to run to the train.

"Now, I generally get something for something," said Minton, as the train thundered in. "Say: 'Good night Gilly,' just as though I wasn't a bloated millionaire."

Jill laughed.

Just as the train moved out, she called genially: "'Good night, Gilly '—"

CHAPTER XX

THE APPLE OF DISCORD

"Whatever is the matter, Janet?"

It was the following afternoon.

This was Jill's inquiry of the Scotchwoman who came into the little blue room, and insisted that she must return to Scotland that very day. Janet was evidently much disturbed.

"It's a family affair, ye ken," said Janet, in an embarrassed way.

"But—what is it?" asked Jill. After a great deal of hesitation, Janet said that her niece Jean, who was not her niece, save by adoption, but quite as much as a niece could be to her, ye ken—had got into trouble.

"She is going to have a baby," said Jill, in the matter of fact way that made her like her father.

"And—he has not wedded her, ye ken," said Janet with difficulty. "An' my brither has turned her away, puir bairn. So I mun gang awa' hame an' see puir Jean."

"The brute!" said Jill. It was not quite clear whether she alluded to Janet's brother or to the man who had not married Jean. Janet chose to think Jill's remark was regarding her brother.

"He's a verra guid man," she said. "Verra strict an' religious."

Jill smiled a little scornfully.

"But can't the man be made to marry Jean?" she inquired. "He has got her into this hole. Let him get her out of it."

Janet shook her head.

"'Tis out o' the question, ye ken," she said, looking dour and sad and very Scotch. Then a faint smile flickered over her face.

"He's in a hole himself, ye ken," she explained. "They buried him in Stanalachan kirkyard a week sin."

"Oh"—said Jill. Her indignation faded.

"But I can't do without you, Janet," she said. "No one can do the housekeeping so well." She paused a moment.

"I have it," she said, in her delighted way when she got what she supposed a good idea.

Janet waited for the idea.

"Jean shall come here," said Jill. "She shall come here and have the baby at Firstlings, Janet, for isn't she a tired mother?"

Janet's eyes filled with slow tears.

"Ye're an angel from aboon," she said, simply. "Ye ken I ken Jean, an' they're braikin' her puir heart. She was a sonsie lassie, aye soft, a little soft, ye ken. But a leal, guid lass, for a' that."

By dinner time it was all arranged. Jean Ferguson was to be sent for, and was to come to Firstlings and be mothered. Janet sent the wire, and received one back from her brother, saying Jean would come, and that he washed his hands of the matter.

"He's hurt, sair," said big-hearted Janet.

"Or he wadna' be sae hard, ye ken. If Rab hadna gane an' deed 't would ha' been different."

Which made Jill smile a little, for Janet was blaming the hapless Rab for dying, rather than her brother for his lack of living charity.

Jean Ferguson arrived at Breezeton on the mid-day train, two days after the wire had been sent.

Jill told Janet she had better go alone to the station to meet her. She saw the two women coming along the road, as she looked out of the bedroom window. When she went down into the hall, Janet and Jean were sitting by the hall fire, on the seat where so many tired mothers had sat. Jill almost wept when she saw Jean's face, the scared look she gave, like a badly hurt animal that has grown to distrust and fear all living things. Jean Ferguson looked almost crazy, as she muttered "Ay," and "Nay," and the droop of her head would have touched any heart. It was settled that she was to help Janet in the kitchen, and as she had been in domestic service, it was thought she would feel a little more independent.

It was some days after Jean's arrival that Jill noticed a vague, indefinite change stealing over the mothers. She allowed it to go on for another day before mentioning it to anyone. Then she tackled Mrs. Williams.

"It's about Jean," said Mrs. Williams.

"Jean!" exclaimed Jill in surprise.

"One of the mothers has been told down in the village that Jean being here will lose them their characters, and make folk think that it's a house for fallen women."

"Fallen women!" gasped Jill, in astonishment.

"Mrs. Clan says she will pack up if there's going to be any stain on her character," said Mrs. Williams. Mrs. Clan was a new arrival.

"You don't like Mrs. Clan, you know," Jill told Mrs. Williams, biting her pencil.

"I don't," admitted Mrs. Williams. "She's one of the take-alls and give nothings. She is not fit to tie that poor girl's boot-strings."

"But—what are we to do?" inquired Jill, in a perturbed way. "I can't turn poor Jean away."

"Turn Mrs. Clan away," said Mrs. Williams.

But Jill would not hear of this.

"It will end one way or the other," said Mrs. Williams, shrewdly. "Mrs. Clan has been too respectable to have any babies herself—even dead ones, and I really don't see that she had a claim to come here."

"She had brought up her brothers and sisters," said Jill. "And has had a hard life."

"Brothers and sisters aren't children," protested Mrs. Williams.

"If she'd only known what I know—seen a little dead face against her breast, she'd have more feeling for poor Jean," she went on.

"Well, she hasn't had them," said Jill, a little irritably. "That gets us nowhere."

Jill could get on the border of falling out with Mrs. Williams, without it weakening their friendship.

That evening the usual concert fell almost flat. The mothers were uneasy. Mrs. Clan had given them fears that the house would get a bad name, and they had nothing, as the Burnley woman said trenchantly, but "what they stood up in" (meaning their clothes) and their good names. It was a situation that anyone with foresight would have seen. The atmosphere was so disturbed that even Jean Ferguson awoke from her own grief to notice it. She was a fair, freckled girl with hair like spun gold, and timid, grey eyes. She was yet a month from being eighteen.

"They want Jean awa'," said Janet, coming into the blue room. "An' Jean has got to feel it in the air. She was just settling doon! Now—she's just ganging in the auld way."

Never had Jill admired the dour Scotchwoman so much. There was not a trace of bitterness in her voice, though her patience and feelings must have been very tried.

"What do you feel about it, Janet?" inquired Jill.

"I think—I canna blame 'em, ye ken. I've sin the day when I'd ha' bin the same myself. But—I've helped to bring Jean Ferguson up, ye ken," answered Janet, simply.

"You mean—you don't judge her," said Jill.

"Judge her!" exclaimed Janet. "I rocked her to sleep when she was a wee bairn."

Jill jumped up from the little chair. She went forward to the plain woman, laid her small hand on each of Janet's broad shoulders and said, "Janet, I love you."

Janet actually blushed.

"Ye ken I canna flatter," she said. "But I like ye weel, Miss Bennett, an' because I dinna want to get you in trouble with the Committee—I'll gang awa' wi' Jean till her time is past." This from the stubborn woman whose nature had been stirred by the attitude of the mothers, was ample proof of her affection for Jill.

"D—A—M—the Committee," was Jill's astounding answer. "We're sticking to Jean, Janet."

"If Mrs. Clan heard ye say damn—" said Janet.

"I have just realised," confessed Jean, "how much easier it is for men not to get hysterical. There are so many words they can use to let off the steam."

"Miss Bennett—" came in very proper tones from the other side of the door.

"Come in," sang Jill, recognising the voice as Mrs. Clan's.

"She's heard ye," said Janet's look.

Mrs. Clan came in. She was a very tall, lanky woman, of bilious appearance, further made noticeable by the redness of her hair. She always dressed in black, because she said it was genteel, but as she had some skin complaint on the legs, she wore white stockings.

"Sit down, Mrs. Clan," Jill invited her, then remembered that there was only Mandy's chair in the room, besides her own. Quite suddenly she got a fear that Mrs. Clan would sit down in dear old Mandy's chair, and desecrate it.

"I do not like Mrs. Clan, either," Jill's subconscious self was saying.

"Oh, sit in my chair," said Jill, aloud, and sat down in Mandy's chair, an elbow on each arm. Immediately she got the feeling that she always got when sitting in that chair, the tender, ridiculous fancy that she was a tiny child, sitting on Mandy's knee, telling all the troubles of her childish day. She grew ashamed of not liking Mrs. Clan. Mrs. Clan sat down in Jill's chair.

The woman evidently expected Jill to open fire. Jill intended to do no such thing.

"I am going home, Miss Bennett," avowed Mrs. Clan. Jill assumed an air of mild surprise.

"Is Mr. Clan sick?" she inquired. Mr. Clan had not the best of health.

"No better and no worse," answered Mrs. Clan. "But he would be if he knew the risks I was running here." She attempted to look like a martyr, but looked a most unholy one, with her closely set eyes and the yellow look.

"Risks?" queried Jill. "Why, there are four fire escapes, and fire-extinguishers all over the place. Whatever do you mean, Mrs. Clan? Don't leave the room, Janet dear." This last sentence was in an utter change of voice.

"I would prefer it," said Janet, looking full to bursting, and speaking English as though she were reading a book.

"Dear Janet—*don't*," begged Jill.

Janet remained in the room ill at ease.

"Now, Mrs. Clan, will you say what risks you ran in staying here?" inquired Jill. "There have been measles in Breezeton, I know, but I am sure you have had measles, and are therefore immune."

"I never had," said Mrs. Clan, thrown off her guard by Jill's apparent innocence.

"Never had measles!" exclaimed Jill in wonder.

"Never had measles," said Mrs. Clan virtuously. "We were too clean. I never had anything."

"Not even children," thought Jill's inner self.

Aloud she only said, "It is very interesting. I had measles. I've had everything."

"Oh—" protested Mrs. Clan, "I was not meaning—"

"The cleanest old woman I ever knew," said Jill pensively, "was a dirty old Irishwoman who turned her red flannel petticoat on Sundays when she went to Mass, and turned it back again afterwards. Flannagan her name was, Bridget Flannagan." Mrs. Clan looked nonplussed.

She had really come into that room to preach quite a sermon, and in imagination had seen Jill sitting very quiet and very small, beseeching her at the end not to leave Firstlings.

"I am sure I have no wish to mention no names," said Mrs. Clan, making a bold dash towards the subject, a dash inspired by her feeling that she was a long way from the goal she had set herself to attain— the housekeeping part at Firstlings, possible only by the exit of Janet Burns.

"Oh, do mention names, Mrs. Clan," said Jill. "Now, supposing you commence by mentioning my name."

Mrs. Clan looked uneasy.

"Or Janet's name," suggested Jill.

Mrs. Clan began to realise that Jill was as cunning as herself.

"Or Jean's name," further suggested Jill. There was a slight flush on her face, and a sparkle in her eye that Mrs. Clan had not realised could burn in those soft depths.

"I have always led a pure life," said Mrs. Clan. "And it is very hard—"

"It always is," said Jill, quickly. "It is only easy for great people, like Jesus Christ, for instance, to live purely. It is hard for you and me, Mrs. Clan."

"God is a spirit," said Mrs. Clan.

She was beginning to look utterly bewildered.

Then she tried to catch on where she had broken off.

"It is very hard to be looked on as a fallen woman," she said, trying to squeeze a tear into those hard eyes of hers. "And I know I do not speak for myself. At least before these evil livers came amongst us—"

"That will do, Mrs. Clan," said Jill.

Her face was more white than Janet Burns', though she was not breathing hard like Janet.

Mrs. Clan quailed before the look in Jill's eyes.

"Jean Ferguson is a good girl," said Jill. "A very good girl, and a very innocent girl, she is not eighteen for a month, yet, Mrs. Clan. Perhaps you have forgotten what you were like when you were only seventeen, though I cannot imagine that even at seventeen you would be so kind-hearted and trusting as Jean was."

Mrs. Clan went paler than either Jill or Janet Burns, and started as though she had been pricked by a needle.

"When I was seventeen—" she stammered, trying to preserve her injured look.

"I have no doubt you were very different from what you are now, Mrs. Clan," said Jill, in a gentle tone.

Mrs. Clan was silent.

The little clock ticked several times. Janet Burns, who was feeling a little faint from the tumult of indignation she had been hurting herself with, advanced towards the blue wall, then remembering that she might grease it, being in her cooking apron, leaned against the door.

Small things sometimes decide great matters. Mrs. Clan, utterly demoralised by the way things were turning out, and disturbed by a supposition that was growing stronger, half imagined in her dementia that Janet Burns was standing against the door to bar her in. It increased her jealousy of Janet. She wanted to hurt Janet badly.

"If my husband had known that I was being asked to sleep under the same roof as a prostitute," she began.

Janet Burns came from her position against the door.

"I'll have ye ken that I rocked Jean Ferguson in her cradle," she began. There was no doubt as to how Janet was going to deal with Mrs. Clan. She did not sing "Scots wha' hae," for nothing.

"Janet, don't speak again," said Jill, calmly. "I am going to deal with Mrs. Clan."

"Prostitutes do not have babies!" said Jill, to Mrs. Clan. "Did you know that?"

"I have never had nothing to do with no prostitutes," said Mrs. Clan. Fear was in her eye, in the tremor of her lashes, the nervous plucking of her dress.

Jill gave her a straight look, a long look. Mrs. Clan lost her head entirely. She gave a half-defensive look back. All that she could think of, see, were Jill's eyes. It is possible that though neither Jill nor she was aware of it, Mrs. Clan was half-hypnotised—self-hypnotised by fear of Jill and Jill's look.

"At least—" she stammered, holding her head up, "Mr. Clan married me."

Had a thunderbolt dropped in the little blue room the other two women could not have been more astounded. There was utter, petrified silence. —

"And *I* was only seventeen," said Mrs. Clan, "and no one took me in and made a god of me. I went to the maternity ward of the workhouse, and they would not give me even a drink of hot tea, though I begged and begged and begged. 'It was against the rules!'"

"Mrs. Clan!" said Jill, "Please—you poor soul!"

Mrs. Clan realised that Jill's eyes were swimming with tears, tears for that seventeen year old girl, going down between the moon-blanched walls, a nurse on each side as she progressed towards the Maternity Ward, afraid, dreadfully afraid, and not a friend near. Tears came into Mrs. Clan's eyes in response to those of Jill's. Then—

"But he married me," she said, striving to regain her morale.

"Jean's lover died," said Jill.

Mrs. Clan turned on Janet Burns.

"Now you can tell them all," she said.

"Noo, I shouldna ha thought on't, "answered Janet, simply. "An' my memory is not ower lang, Mrs. Clan. What ye've said just the noo has ganged in at one ear and ganged oot at tither. Tis a proverb o' mine that we puir women folk should stan' by one anither in our troubles an' trials. God knows the men folk are aye thick in the head—or the heart, never having bin mithers the noo. Dry your ee' the noo, Mrs. Clan. And believe me—"

It was almost dramatic.

Jill as well as Mrs. Clan wondered what was coming at Janet's pause.

"I think the better o' ye, noo, ye ken, than ever I did before," said Janet.

Then Janet and Mrs. Clan began to talk, until Jill was almost deafened. But it was friendly talk.

"Someone's knocking," said Jill, for the second time, in the midst of the row.

Janet opened the door.

"Three of the other's have packed up," said the Burnley woman. "I'm willing to stay, provided things are made clear. I don't want nobody calling me no fallen woman—or I'll take one half of their face off. So—let's get to the bottom on it."

It was sound common-sense. Janet, Mrs. Robinson and Mrs. Clan filed out.

"I'm coming, Janet," said Jill.

She leaned her head on her hand for a moment when they had gone.

"Oh, Mandy, why did you die?" her Irish heart was saying. She believed that Mandy could have settled it all in five minutes, as probably she could.

"It's a weary thing being a mother," thought Jill, drawing a deep breath. Her head was almost splitting, and she was void of an idea, could form no plan how to deal with all those mothers waiting in the big common room for the reason of their having to carry the suspicion that some of them were not "all as they should be."

"I must trust to inspiration, and the fact that there's an orator on the family tree," mused Jill ruefully, and went out of the little room, towards the loud hum made by the voices of respectable British matrons justly annoyed that they might be suspected of being fallen women.

CHAPTER XXI

HEARTS ARE TRUMPS

WHEN Jill entered the Common Room the buzz of noise made by some score of women who were talking in little groups of twos, threes, and fours, ceased, at once. It was plain to see that there was division in the camp, though all the women looked somewhat uncomfortable. Jill had heard one speech amidst the general hub-bub, just as she opened the door, and had recognised the voice as proceeding from a pale-faced woman whom she had taken a great fancy to on first seeing. Nancy Shaw was from a colliery district and had been a pitbrow worker. The words she had spoken were a keynote to her character, as well as to the situation aroused by Jean Ferguson's coming, and the Breezeton gossips.

"I'd sooner be thought ill on than do ill," had been Nancy Shaw's comment. "We've our own consciences, and nobody can pinch them. But I think somebody ought to see that Breezeton woman as is setting out this is a house for the fallen, and put a spoke in her little wheel, and I think things should be made clear in the "Breezeton Courier,"—just to circumcise aught 'at anyone can say."

It was the expression "circumcise," that made Jill hang back a moment before entering the room, in order to control her amusement. She knew that Nancy, who was fond of long words, meant circumvent. The humorous side of the situation was apparent to Jill, after Nancy's speech, though she still realised it as serious.

Jill's entrance had the effect that is common when grievances are to be discussed. Those who had had most to say went back into their shells, and found it difficult to say anything, which made those who had been more timid rather disgusted.

When Mrs. Clan, who had been the instigator of the whole, uneasiness was seen to be taking what the Burnley woman called "a back seat" in the affair, there were many indignant glances cast in her direction. They knew that she had gone in to see Jill, telling them that she was not going to stand it, and had come out—like a wet rag, as the Burnley woman whispered to Nancy Shaw.

"Where are the three who are packing up?" asked Jill. "Will someone tell them they are wanted."

Mrs. Robinson went. Jill waited until the three appeared. It was pretty obvious that they did not want to leave Firstlings, really, but had felt genuine concern about the rumours being circulated.

"Janet, would you mind seeing to the tea and cakes coming in at four?" asked Jill, lightly.

The hall clock struck half-past three just as Janet Burns moved across the common room, knowing quite well that Jill had sent her out of the way. In half-an-hour Jill apparently hoped to straighten out the tangle.

"Suppose we all sit down," said Jill, suiting the action to the word.

"It's as cheap sitting as standing," agreed Nancy Shaw.

The mothers all sat down. Each basket chair held a mother. Jill sat on the floor, which made her look more like a little girl than ever.

"Now about Jean Ferguson and this risk you run of being thought fallen women," said Jill.

She had entirely dropped the idea of depending on the Irish orator for inspiration. Jill was feeling very English and responsible. She could not laugh at the mothers' concern about their getting a bad name. They looked as worried as she felt.

"It was Jane Riley told Mrs. Clan folk would think it a house for the fallen," said Nancy Shaw.

"Have you looked on this place, each of you, as your own home?" inquired Jill.

There was a murmur of assent.

"If one night a poor girl, turned out by the people who had adopted her, came knocking on your door,— with no place to lay her head," Jill went on, stressing these words, "would any single one of you turn her away? Would you not rather take her in, and mother her? Jean is only just over seventeen. Some of you have girls about that age."

"I've one just gone seventeen. Taller nor her father, she is," chirped Nancy Shaw.

Jill could have blessed her. Without being conscious of it she was like an accompaniment to all Jill said, making an appeal that Jill could not have made— because Jill was not a working woman.

"I've one'll be that come Febooary," said another.

"Well, what are we to do with Jean? She is in your hands," Jill told them. "Now before you decide, I want you to know all the story." Sitting with her hands clasped around her knees, Jill told them the simple story, as she had pieced it together from what Janet told her. Jean, and Rab, and the religious father, whose religion blocked the way of common human kindness— the mothers saw them all, with the background of the

Scottish solitudes. So the Irish orator had come up after all.

"It isn't as we judge her," said Nancy Shaw, who would probably have been surprised to know that she was more clear-headed and concise than many a British statesman. "It isn't that, Miss Bennett. It's because folk is judging us through it. I'll not be muck under anybody's nose." There was universal approval of this sentiment. "We want clearing. Why, look, if the pedlar gets hold o' the tale as this house is for the fallen, it'll go all round them there hills—" pointing at the long line seen from the window, "and out o' one dale into t'other—till th' King an' Queen'll hear on it up at London. An' it'll not lose naught, neither."

Apparently there had been an orator in Nancy Shaw's family.

Every gaze was now on Jill, asking her how she would answer that argument, and it was, strongly felt that Nancy Shaw, who had had less to say against Jean being at Firstlings, than anybody, was putting the case well for the mothers. They would have been greatly astonished had they known that Jill was finding Nancy very helpful. Without her there would have been no free expression.

"I propose," said Jill, "that we send for Jane Riley."

"She wouldn't come," chirped the Burnley woman, who knew working-class psychology better than Jill. "If I'd been scandalising folk, would I go to face 'em?" she inquired. "'Tisn't a vestry meeting. I propose as we all goes down to see Jane Riley."

"All?" inquired Jill. "Why not four representatives?"

"My Tom has seen representatives," said the Burnley woman, wisely. "I say, let's all go."

Jill laughed. She could not help it. She wondered how all the mothers would get into Jane Riley's small kitchen. Then, the irresistible humour of the thing overbalanced her sense of the correct thing to do.

"We'll go now," said Jill. "But let us have a clear cut plan. Twenty women can't talk at once."

It was unanimously decided that Nancy Shaw should be spokeswoman.

"I'm coming, too," Jill told them. "Just to preserve law and order." There was a general laugh. Firstlings saw a great bustle of mothers getting hats and coats on.

When they got out upon the road they met the old postman, the same whom Mandy had used to look at suspiciously, when he said he had no letters from London, just as though she thought he had pocketted them.

"Is Jane Riley at home?" queried Jill.

He looked a little surprised.

"Ay," he said, "Is it her 'At Home' day?"

Jill laughed.

"Have you seen the pedlar?" she inquired casually.

"Jane were having a yarn with him about summat," he said.

The mothers strove to hide their despair. The postman went on.

"I can see the pedlar," said Jill. "Now, Nancy, you go on to Jane, get the names of every person she has slandered Jean to as a fallen woman. I'm after the pedlar."

Jill set out at a run. She had on a hobble skirt, and occasionally it a'most tripped her up. The first house from Jane Riley's cottage was a farm two hundred yards away. The pedlar had got a good start.

"Go on, Nancy," said Mrs. Robinson. "We'll stand on this hill and watch the race."

It certainly was exciting to watch Jill trying to catch the pedlar, who was a lithe, strong man for all his forty pounds weight pack. Moreover, the pedlar had done the worst part of the hill road. It was almost perpendicular at one point.

"She's gaining on him," said Mrs. Robinson.

"Go on, Jill. I'm backing Jill," she added. Mrs. Robinson could never forget that she had once been at the Derby with "our Tom."

"No. He's going to do it," said' a pessimist.

"She's having a rest."

It was true something had happened to Jill's suspender.

"She's pulling her stocking up," said Mrs. Clan timidly.

Mrs. Robinson gave her a furious glance.

"You old tomcat," she said," If it had not been for you the poor little thing wouldn't had to be winding herself like this."

"I only said what Jane Riley said," murmured Mrs. Clan.

"Jill's gaining on him," said another. It was the first time they had called her Jill. They really knew that she was one of them now.

"I couldn't run like that to save my life," said one.

"She's running to save our good names," said another. "Eh, she nearly tumbled, then."

"The pedlar's stopped," said one woman.

"Nay "—said the other. For the two figures were getting smaller and yet more small.

It was at this moment that one of the women spied Janet Burns, hatless, and in her tea-apron, speeding towards them, looking distracted.

"The pedlar has stopped," said one of the mothers. "Thank the Lord."

It was true. He had turned to look back, and had seen Jill, whom he did not recognise, waving her handkerchief. Her hair was down, so was her stocking, and horrible thing, she had split the hobble-skirt. He never forgot the dialogue they had, just by the old thorn-tree that tradition said had been a gallows-tree. Jill held her rent skirt together all the time they spoke.

"Sit down and get your wind, Miss Jill," he advised, when he recognised her. But Jill would not.

"Is this the first call you have made since you were in Jane's house?" asked Jill, panting. Her heart went thump, thump against her side, and the blood was singing in her ears.

When he nodded, she sat down.

The pedlar heard her out.

"I should not have passed it on," he said. "I've bin picking a crow with Jane myself, about something she told about my lass. And if the tale does meet me anywhere—if she's told anyone else—I'll tell 'em the true tale, as you've just told it me. A bit o' gossip's all right, but Jane's the limit."

"Then I've burst my suspender for nothing," said Jill. She had known the pedlar from being a tiny child. The pedlar watched her go down the hill-road again, shaking his head at intervals as though to say there was a girl for you! Doctor Bennett had pulled the pedlar's wife through several severe illnesses, and it was common belief that Breezeton churchyard held several it would not have got so soon had he been living.

When Jill got down to the group of women who had watched her race, Janet Burns had vanished again, and with her the Burnley woman.

"It's that poor girl," they told Jill.

"She's in labour. Premature, poor thing. It's all she's gone through brought it on."

They trudged back to Firstlings, Firstlings that seemed different, somehow, with the angels of Life and Death trying to get into that little room where Janet Burns and the Burnley woman waited for the doctor.

"Don't come in. You're too young," Janet told Jill, when she tapped lightly on the door.

"Please—" asked Jill.

They let her in. She was astonished to find Jean sitting on one of the little white chairs. She looked like a frightened child, but she was making no moan.

"It's the Scotch in her," said Janet, proudly.

Jill went out and down into the little blue room. She carried out of it her own little chair, and the fat cushion stool, and took them into Jean Ferguson's room.

"Dinna fash yoursel'," Janet told her.

"But the claes—ye ken the bairn will want some claes," she added.

Jill went out again. The mothers were all in the Common Room, but how changed from the women who had looked so anxious about their good names going. Nancy Shaw stood in their midst, telling how she had dealt with Jane Riley—and how Jane Riley had almost gone down on her bended knees when Nancy threatened a libel suit. It was all over, the trouble that had looked such an insurmountable thing. The mothers were themselves again. In five minutes they were all talking away at sixty miles an hour, comparing notes as to how they had been when in the same place as poor Jean, and Jill went out to bring in the tea and cakes they had forgotten.

"Don't mind me," said Jill, smiling, when one of them stopped midway in a sentence. "My father was a doctor."

"Well, all here are wed or going mad to be," said Nancy Shaw, "so I don't see as it matters."

As Jill was the only single woman there was a laugh at her expense, in which she joined heartily.

"The doctor," said a mother, as the bell rung.

Jill went to let him in. She took him up to the little room, and rejoined the mothers.

When he had gone, she went up and tapped on the door again.

Janet looked up.

"She'll be dree an' lang," she said, soberly. "But you're my ain brave lass, Jeanie." The poor child held Janet's hand.

It was dree and long. The mothers were used to going to bed at nine, but sat up waiting. At ten the bell rang.

"It will be Giles back from town with the clothes," said Jill. For Giles had been commissioned to go to town, and Nancy Shaw herself had written out the list of little garments required.

Giles came up into the Common Room, and the parcel was opened, the mothers standing all round. It was a picture worthy of a great painter, those working-class mothers pressing round to see the little garments, the firelight and shadow flickering over their faces.

"One, two, three, four woollen shirts. Them's right," proclaimed Nancy.

"Mercy on me, where's the skips?" asked the Burnley woman.

"Ships?" inquired old Giles stupidly.

"Skips, man, skips," corrected the Burnley woman. She turned a sad look on the rest of the mothers.

"They've gien him all barrows," she said.

"Barrows!" exclaimed old Giles, who could only think of wheel-barrows from association of ideas.

"Was it a chap served you?" asked the Burnley woman.

Giles nodded.

"Ay, I'll bet it was," said Nancy Shaw. "What do they know?"

"Eight barrows an' no skips," said Mrs. Clan. "Well, we shall have to make some. We could do it in an hour." Which suggestion helped to put her right with the mothers.

"Safety pins," said one. "Are there safety pins?"

"Ten sheets," said Giles, happily.

"I wrote two," exclaimed Nancy Shaw. "And I'm sure my writing's plain as daylight."

"There's two sets o' binders here," said another mother. Never had Jill seen them so happy. They jostled and pushed, and felt at everything, and took the tickets off, and set the things to air.

"Shops are damp," said Mrs. Clan.

There was a murmur of assent. It was queer to see the tiny things hanging round the common room fire, turned by first one woman and another. They felt they had something to make up to Jean, and Mrs. Clan seemed to feel it more than anyone.

Jill met her on the stairs, taking a hot drink up to the little room.

"What was your baby called?" Jill asked Mrs. Clan, referring to the stillborn child born in that Maternity Ward of the Workhouse three and thirty years ago.

"Amelia," said Mrs. Clan. Her voice shook a little. Then she said, "That child'll be cold, when its born, being premature. We should ha' some cotton wool."

"We haven't any cotton wool," said Jill. "Unless we take the stuffings out of an eiderdown." Which was what they did. The mothers were up into midnight, finishing the skips, which they made half the usual size, and the little eiderdown coats.

When the hall clock struck twelve Jill ordered them to bed.

Jill sat up all through the long night. She put a fire in the little blue room, the first that had burnt there, cold though the weather had been, and as she allowed the fire in the Common Room to die down, she took away the tiny garments for Jean Ferguson's baby, hanging them around her fire. She drew up Mandy's chair, and sat waiting, hearing the mothers settle down, with something of the feelings a tired mother of many children might have.

As she saw the little garments, it was not strange that Jill's childish dream about the babies she would have, came back to her, like a dream, dreamed long long ago. She had used to tell Mandy that she could have twenty-five children—twenty girls and five boys! A whimsical smile stole over her face, and she leaned forwards to turn one of the tiny shirts that really did not need it. Then she handled a pair of woollen socks. They looked as though they had come out of fairyland, so wee they were, as they stood on her hand.

"Out of some sweat-shop, more likely," mused Jill. "But who would think it?"

Janet Burns coming down for hot water, saw the light in Jill's room, and came in.

"Lang an' drear. It may arrive by daylight," she answered Jill's questioning look.

Jill's eyes filled with tears.

"Have you chosen a name, Janet," she asked.

"Rab, if it's a man child," Janet told her.

"After a', the man couldna help deein', if his time had come. And Jean's forgi'en him the wrang."

Jill saw that Janet had striven hard to forgive Rab, and had done it.

"If it's a girl—?" questioned Jill.

"She's ca'in' it after you," said Janet, beaming.

"Jill Amelia, then," said Jill.

"Weel—it'll not go ill wi' Ferguson," said Janet, giving way again.

Jill continued to sit by the fire turning the little garments. She was half tumbling asleep, at seven in the morning, when Janet's knock falling on the door made her give a startled cry.

"Janet!"

"Here 'tis," said Janet, and brought in what looked like a big white shawl, that was stirring a little, and from which proceeded a muffled cry.

"Mrs. Robinson 'll wash it," she told Jill.

Jill gasped, peeping at the little creature, as Janet unfolded the shawl.

"She never will," said Jill, determinedly. "She'll hurt it."

So the baby was washed in the little blue room by Jill and Janet.

"It might gang easily inside one of them blue quart jugs ye ha, Miss Jill," said Janet, proudly.

"Jill Amelia Ferguson, hush your din, don't ye ken ye're Scotch?"

"It ought to bring us luck," said Jill.

"They allus bring guid luck," said Janet.

What a breakfast time it was next morning. Mrs. Clan made breakfast, and a fine old muddle it was, but nobody minded, and afterwards one by one, they were admitted to the shrine of the baby.

When Mrs. Clan learned that the baby's second name was Amelia—she forgave Jean Ferguson for having been made a god of in her trouble, whilst she had been treated to official charity.

The days that followed were great days at Firstlings. The mothers took turns at staying up all night with the baby, which needed feeding every hour—three teaspoonsful a time. Jean Ferguson was not allowed to give the child milk, being yet so sad and heart-crushed that the doctor feared the child would have convulsions from mother's milk.

"It's ma brither, ye ken," said Janet Burns.

Which decided Jill to set out to the town one stormy sunset, to send a wire to that obdurate brother. Janet had apparently given him up.

It was a long walk. Dusk fell before Jill left Breezeton, and she knew that it would be a headlong race to get the wire through. She got into a crowded post office ten minutes before closing time, and addressed the telegram to Adam Anderson. Her message was very simple.

"Jean at death's door. A fine daughter—Janet."

The address of Firstlings was wired also.

"There!" said Jill to herself. "It's a lie, and its forgery. I hope the end justifies the means."

It was almost a black night when she left the lamplit streets behind, and got upon the Breezeton road. She walked into a horse- trough and scrambled out again wet to the knees. The superstition that came from the land of banshees and fairies gave her fears of every tree. She thought in a tired muddled way of Mason and Firstlings. That was quite sound now, financially. Mrs. Williams could manage it for her. She was very tired when she got in, and the mothers had got alarmed at the lateness of the hour.

"Is it late?" asked Jill.

"Eleven," they told her.

"But I left town at eight," said Jill, "and I've walked hard."

She was puzzled at its having taken her three hours to reach Firstlings. She was more than tired. She went to bed and slept, and next day was too tired to get up. The day after she crawled down to her post, and sat in the blue room.

"I must really have walked slow, though I thought I was going fast," Jill solved the problem of those hours from town to Breezeton. "I am run down. I will go off to the moors." But in the afternoon she felt too tired to go to the moors.

"Someone at the door, Janet," she told Janet, at three that afternoon. All the rest were out, having gone to see a curious old church some miles distant.

Janet went. Jill caught the startled exclamation, and listened.

"I got your wire, Janet," said a man's voice. "How is Jean?"

Jill trembled.

Was it to be a charge of forgery, or would she go down to posterity as a peacemaker?

"Dinna say she's gane, Janet," said the man's voice. Janet grasped the situation.

"She's just taken a turn yesterday," she told her brother. "An' the bairn is just Jean ower again, like she was when ye foun' her amang the heather. And ye could stick her in a quart mug."

"But ye said she was a fine bairn," said Adam.

"She's a pair o' lungs," said Janet." Come up, man, but ye'd better take off your shoes."

"No," shouted Jill, making them both start. "Go up just as you are, Mr. Anderson."

It was a complete reconciliation. Jean was to go home with her baby and there was forgiveness on each side, and perhaps a deeper love than there had ever been. Janet Burns asked Jill where she expected to go to for such tricks—but Janet was well pleased.

That night Jill waited up for the mothers.

Now that all was settled, Jill realised how excited she really was. The room felt as though it swayed sometimes, as though she were on a ship.

After boiling the milk and setting all the glasses ready on the tray, Jill felt suddenly chill. There was always a roaring fire in the hall, though they had endeavoured lately to economise on some of the other fires. Now, they would not need to economise. She could have twice as many mothers at the place. It was all like a wonderful dream. Firstlings was saved, and Jean Ferguson was going to be happy.

Jill walked out of the kitchen, into the hall, all rosy with the fire. She sat down on the seat where the first lot of tired mothers had sat, and realised just how tired she was. The mothers had been having a little concert.

The party was breaking up.

She could hear Janet Burns saying that she must boil the milk and decided to go and tell her there was no need to boil it, that it was already boiled. But Jill felt strangely lazy. She tried to make herself move but could not.

"Supper is ready," cried Mrs. Williams, coming into the hall at that moment.

Jill tried to say something.

She found she could not speak. It was like a nightmare when one was awake. Mrs. Williams must have seen that something was wrong. She came nearer.

Mrs. Williams, the diminutive, became alarmingly magnified. She was quite a giantess. Jill believed that she, Jill Bennett, must have turned into Alice in Wonderland, and had hazy notions that Alice in Wonderland must be founded on fact—when she felt everything swim around her.

Mrs. Williams just reached the chair in time.

"I think," said Jill, in what sounded like a very loud voice, "I am going to be ill."

As a matter of fact she made no sound. Only her lips moved, and Mrs. Williams called loudly for aid, and a rush of mothers answered the call. They closed round Jill like the waves of the sea. It was the six-foot Mrs. Robinson from Burnley who carried Jill into her room like a baby.

"Mrs. Morgan, you've done ambulance work," someone said.

Mrs. Morgan followed Mrs. Robinson into the little white room.

"She's got a temperature," she said. "We should get a doctor."

"Let me go," said Mrs. Robinson.

She went out into a world that was all mist and darkness with a look that said she would carry a doctor under her arm if he did not move quickly enough.

"Hello, what's this?" said Mrs. Morgan. She opened a letter from the executors of the solicitor from whom Jill had borrowed. She read it. It was a threat—a threat that the furniture would be removed from Firstlings if Jill did not return the five hundred pounds.

"Here, stop that," cried Mrs. Williams.

Mrs. Morgan flashed out in her true colours. She had appeared a shy woman before.

"Can she look after her own affairs?" she asked scornfully. "Don't I look on her as my own daughter?"

Mrs. Williams' wrath died down, and the tears sprang to her eyes. The cat was out. Outside clustered all the mothers, who would get to know the straits Firstlings had been in from Mrs. Morgan, if she did not tell them. So then, on the little landing, by light of the candles, Mrs. Williams told them the story simply.

"She went into debt for us," murmured one, as if that was the sum total of human sacrifice.

"I'm going," said one ingrate, "if the bums are coming. I'm not used to that." She was overvoiced and shamed in a moment. The mothers were all calling out with one voice, "We'll see her through." Mrs. Williams looked at them. To tell them of the millionaire's gift to Firstlings was to rob them of the joy of being real shipmates in Firstlings. Mrs. Williams let them think that Firstlings was on the rocks, and that they were to pull it round. After all, was that not what Fellowship meant, and what a joy to give to Jill, when Jill got better, and then Jill could tell them all was well, and—thank them.

The government of Firstlings by the mothers began in good earnest. Janet Burns became Secretary, by democratic vote, and the Burnley woman took her place in the kitchen. Mrs. Williams and Mrs. Morgan looked after Jill whilst Jill Amelia Ferguson slept and fed, fed and slept, clad in the eiderdown jackets Jill had made, and the door knocker of Firstlings was muffled lest it disturb Jill the elder.

Jill was terribly ill. Collapse, the doctor called it.

There were great confabs every night in the common room. Everybody spoke in hushed voices. It was agreed that those whose time had expired should return, saying nothing to anyone of the financial crisis at Firstlings!

Meanwhile everybody tried to keep down expenses.

"Porridge is fine, do ye ken?" said Janet, and porridge became the rule at Firstlings for breakfast.

Between them they washed and cleaned. There was not a branch of work at Firstlings but someone could do it. Mrs. Robinson even cobbled their shoes—cobbling as quickly as possible, and as far away from that room where J ill lay still as possible, whilst the mothers stood around, amusingly admiring every nail that went in, and so surprised to find that they could walk in the shoes when cobbled.

The mothers had never had so happy a time as when they were allowed in this large, beautiful house, to do all the scheming and planning and dreaming that they had done in the little ugly houses. Which would have upset Jill very much—only she could not know, being terribly self-centred and raving of Mandy and Mason, and owing money to Benson's, and whether or not Firstlings would ever be used as an orphanage.

The mothers were mothering Jill. They realised also that the letter from Mr. Wicks must be answered one way or the other.

Mr. Wicks had said, "Since you care for the young man, why not marry him?" Mrs. Robinson took that literally.

"Seeing she can't answer for hersel', we'll ha' to write for her," said the Burnley woman. So they sent word that Jill would marry Mason, if she lived to marry him. Mr. Wicks went to see Will.

He found that young man surrounded by luggage, and with a look on his face that said if he got off he would never come back.

On reading the letter he changed his viewpoint, and his clothes, and Mr. Wicks went to Euston and saw him off.

He travelled all night, arriving at Breezeton as the brickworkers got on the train for their day's work.

Jill was perhaps dying. That was the thought beating in his brain.

Jill, who had been making him more angry at her silly pride than anything ever had done, or could do, was perhaps dead now. The intolerably long journey was met by the disappointment of finding the vehicle that went past Firstlings had just departed. He had to walk, and walked to such purpose that he passed the vehicle. He almost reeled when he saw that the blinds were not down at Firstlings. Jill was alive yet.

CHAPTER XXII

AT THE ELEVENTH HOUR

It was Janet Burns who met Will Mason in the hall.

"I ken ye're the man," said she.

"How is she?" asked Mason.

Janet cast a glance at his face. Whatever "doots "she had of Jill's being in love with him, no one could have any of his being in love with Jill.

"Weel," said Janet, "th' doctor says she's na chance at a'. But ye ken, doctors are only human folk, ye ken— an' these lean folk tak' a muckle killin'."

Mason stared into the cautious Scottish face. Jill had no mother.

He sat down and told Janet Burns all about it.

"Ye ken, from what she lets fa', ye'll be her guid man," said Janet. Then, feeling she had said too much, she added, cautiously: "If *she disna dee, ye ken*."

The struggle to win Jill through to life became more grim. Curiously enough, it was Mrs. Williams who had the most soothing effect on her. That little Welshwoman did not spare herself. As Janet Burns said, there must have been "a strong point to her somewhere," for she got little sleep.

Mason took lodgings at the old inn. He wrote to Mr. Wicks that Jill and he were to get married. But he said nothing of the documentary evidence.

This on the eighth day. There were only two more days to bring it to the ten-day limit set by Uncle Birch's will.

On the ninth day Jill took a turn.

On the morning of the tenth she said, in a ghost of a voice, to Mrs. Williams, "Who is that speaking?"

"Mr. Mason," said Mrs. Williams.

"Oh!" said Jill, without surprise.

"Would you like to see him?" quoth Mrs. Williams.

There was a short pause.

"Yes" said Jill at length.

The doctor came in just then. He was consulted.

Mason was given ten minutes. He came in.

"Have you been ill?" asked Jill weakly.

Mason shook his head. He had a drawn, worn look.

The little room was decorated for Yule.

Jill's hair was cut short.

"I—put Firstlings in pawn," said Jill.

Mason nodded.

It was strange to see Jill so helpless and—so childishly yielding. For, without the least thing being said, that much was apparent.

"What would *you* do?" asked Jill.

She did not even fear that he would think she was altering her other verdict. She knew him for her friend, her best friend, having no ideas about the "bargain" that had roused her Irish blood "against" him.

"It is out of pawn," he said.

He told her about the millionaire. She had forgotten the episode.

"You are going abroad—?" queried Jill.

For five minutes they talked of Firstlings, of Mandy, the mothers, and—he did not tell Jill that the mothers knew, or what they had done. She forgot to ask how he had got to know that she was sick.

"Your mother will feel sorry you are going," said Jill.

"Very," acknowledged Mason.

Another two minutes went.

"I sail on Thursday," said Mason.

Jill went even paler. He had not supposed she could do so.

"Time's up," said a voice outside the door.

"Good-bye," said Mason.

"Good-bye," faltered Jill.

He knew he could have broken her will by the exertion of his now. But it would have been like a Titan wrestling with a child. He did not want to win her that way.

He held out his hand. Jill's tiny one just touched it. He knew she was struggling. He made no effort to retain it. And he did not look at her.

"Good-bye," said Jill quietly.

He walked across to the room door. His hand was on the knob.

"Will!" said Jill, sitting up in bed.

His name was only whispered, but he was back in one stride.

Jill was sobbing on his shoulder, sobbing out her broken pride, her care, the weight of Firstlings, ebbing away from her.

"And I—I have something to tell you," she said, between the sobs. "I—did—not—bury—him. He—jilted—me—and then I had to. I just hated you to know, somehow."

"Mrs. Greenwall told me," said Mason. "If you like, Jill, I will knock him down. Anyhow, I guessed all the time. Lucky for me, Jill, that he did not hold tight."

The knocking on the door became imperative.

Mason took out his watch.

"There is just time to get a wire through to save *our* money," he said.

Jill did not even ask him anything about it, or wince at the mention of money.

"Back soon!" he said buoyantly.

Mr. Wicks got the first satisfactory wire at the eleventh instant.

"Jill has promised," Mason wired; "documentary evidence follows."

And Mr. Wicks heaved a big sigh of relief.

*****

Firstlings had a merry Christmas. But Jill was not there. Jill was in Devon, feeling more of a child than ever she had done in her life. Will Mason's mother was even nicer than he was, Jill told him, quite candidly.

Mrs. Williams was left in charge. She was to take Jill's place permanently at some future time.

Which she did, in the spring, when Jill and Mason "set up" in a pretty flat overlooking Hampstead Heath.

A year afterwards the scheme was adopted as quite a fixture. Mr. Williams was working in the neighbourhood. The old "young committee" had vanished, some of it being married; its place was taken by an older committee, composed of some of that lot of mothers who believed *sub rosa*, that they had pulled Firstlings—and Jill—through. Children were to be allowed to come with the mothers—to a limited degree, of course.

Jill was agreeable to that now. She had a fat baby of her own, aged one month, who, she vowed, was "taking notice." Mrs. Williams told Jill, after a time, that another house mother must be got.

"Nonsense!" said Jill. "There'll be room for you just the same—and—why should you go away, anyhow?"

When Baby Williams arrived it was as even Mason admitted, a "very fine baby "—with a reservation, of course. As for Mrs. Williams—she was almost wild with the joy of a living baby!

Firstlings is still progressing, and even getting known in other countries. In the place where cabbages used to be grown there is a big grass-plot sacred to "Babies," and every year Jill takes her boy to roll on it, in company with other babies, and everybody is happy, and there are no more mothers wanting to go home before the time is up.

Every year Giles comes at Christmastide, with his simple gifts, for Jill always spends Yule there, and Santa Claus is very busy indeed, bringing so much to Firstlings that it is hard to believe he has anything left for any other place.

The very sanest person does not dare to say now that Firstlings is a mistake—a mad, Jillish mistake. But Jill knows it for what it is—a tiny "making-up" for the grey lives endured by those whose work is the most important in the world—the work that some have called Soul-Making. Some day, she hopes, there will be no need of places like Firstlings.

THE END